FALSE ENCHANTMENT

Cheshire, 1659. Rose Kingsley's widowed mother has lost her farm and now they must live in a cottage, scratching a living somehow. Into Rose's life comes farmer R chard Overton, who asks her to marry him. But before she can give him her answer, Lady Stretton offers her the chance to work in London as a lady's maid. Rose decides to take-up the offer and then return to Richard, but things go disastrously wrong when she is introduced to the unscrupulous Lord Wilde . . .

Books by Sheila Holroyd
in the Linford Romance Library:

ALL FOR LOVE
THE FACE IN THE MIRROR
DISTANT LOVE
FLIGHT TO FREEDOM

SHEILA HOLROYD

◆

FALSE ENCHANTMENT

Complete and Unabridged

LINFORD
Leicester

First published in Great Britain

First Linford Edition
published 2001

British Library CIP Data

Holroyd, Sheila
  False enchantment.—Large print ed.—
  Linford romance library
  1. Love stories
  2. Large type books
  I. Title
  823.9'14 [F]

ISBN 0–7089–9738–4

Published by
F. A. Thorpe (Publishing)
Anstey, Leicestershire

Set by Words & Graphics Ltd.
Anstey, Leicestershire
Printed and bound in Great Britain by
T. J. International Ltd., Padstow, Cornwall

This book is printed on acid-free paper

1

If Alice Wright had not tried to break the eggs, Rose Kingsley would not have been saved by Richard Overton, and the future of all three would have been very different! Alice should not have given in to the malicious impulse, especially when she was trying to convince Richard what a pleasant companion she was as they strolled through the weekly market in the Cheshire village of Frotesham.

As usual, the market was a cheerful hubbub as customers carefully examined the produce offered to them by local farmers and cottagers who had managed to grow a little more than their hungry families needed. Then Alice saw Rose making her way through the crowd, carefully guarding a covered basket, and guessed that it contained eggs which Rose and her mother had decided they could exchange for a few coins. Doubtless she was looking for a friendly stallholder who would add them to his own stock.

The temptation was irresistible. As Rose turned her head to look at a stall, Alice stuck out her foot and Rose tripped over it. The basket with the precious eggs would have gone flying if Richard Overton had not acted so swiftly, leaping forward to gather both Rose and the basket in his arms. Shocked and startled, Rose clutched the basket with one arm and his neck with the other, and he found himself gazing down into big, pansy-brown eyes. The colour rose to her cheeks as he set her down carefully.

'Thank you,' she said gratefully.

'Did you hurt yourself?'

She shook her head, busy checking the contents of the basket.

'You saved me. Anyway, a couple of bruises wouldn't have mattered. The important thing is that the eggs are safe!'

'What a relief!' Alice commented patronisingly.

Rose turned.

'Good morning, Alice — Mistress Alice,' she amended as Alice's eyebrows rose haughtily.

The other girl responded with a curt nod, while Richard looked from one to another. Both wore plain grey dresses with white collars and caps, as befitted the England of 1659, but Alice Wright, daughter of a well-to-do farmer, wore a carefully-made gown in a good, woollen fabric which was obviously fairly new. Her fine linen collar and cap had discreet lace edging. In contrast, Rose's gown showed its age and poor quality, and her collar and cap were those which a maid-servant might have worn. Alice's gown fitted her full figure perfectly, while Rose was evidently out-growing hers.

Alice laid a possessive hand on Richard's sleeve.

'Shall we go on? I still have things to buy.'

A little taken aback by her discourtesy to the other girl, Richard hesitated, but Rose gave him a quick smile.

'I must get these sold safely before I have another accident,' she informed him. 'Thank you again.'

With that, she was gone, leaving Richard to look after her with curiosity.

'Who was that?' he enquired, as he and Alice resumed their progress.

'That awkward girl? Her name is Rose Kingsley. Her father was a tenant farmer near Frotesham, but he was sadly impoverished and when he died last year he left his family with nothing. Someone else wanted to rent the farm, so Rose and her mother had to leave. The steward of the estate kindly let her take over a cottage with a plot of land in the lee of Frotesham Hill in return for a tiny rent, so they live there now, scratching a living somehow.'

'So now she must call you Mistress Alice and not Alice,' he commented.

She shrugged her shoulders.

'It is more fitting. She is no longer

my equal, and as a girl without a dowry she is not likely to make a good marriage and rise to her former position. She must learn to show respect to her superiors.'

Richard reflected that the girl by his side might be pretty, and have the extra advantage of being the heiress to a fine farm, but she was revealing some unpleasant aspects of her nature as she grew more confident of his growing interest in her.

His own farm lay some five miles nearer Chester, and it was in that city that he had encountered Alice for the first time when she had accompanied her father in order to see what Chester had to offer that Frotesham's few shops did not. Master Wright was an acquaintance, and when he had seen Richard's admiration of Alice's looks he had reminded himself that Richard would make a good match and had invited the young man to call when he was next near Frotesham. At twenty-five, Richard had begun to think of marriage, and Alice had seemed a very possible future partner at that first meeting, so he had made it his business to visit Master Wright and his family soon after.

He had been warmed by his welcome. His life was spent in hard work and most of the time he saw only his mother and the labourers who worked for him, so a close family circle in a house which was furnished for comfort as well as use was a pleasant change. Now, after half-a-dozen visits, he reflected that it might be wise to stay away for a while. He was not yet ready to commit himself, and he did not want to have an angry Master Wright claiming that he had misled his daughter as to his intentions. With this in mind, he left unexpectedly early that day, and Alice was unable to make him change his mind.

'What is the matter?' she pouted as he mounted his horse. 'Surely you could stay till nearer evening.'

He smiled down at her, but remained

firm in spite of her persuasions.

'I have work to do, and I am expecting a cow to calve soon. It is her first, so I want to be there.'

She frowned, annoyed that he was able to resist her.

'Go then, if you must. I trust we shall see you again soon.'

He rode away, relieved to have escaped, and when he realised these feelings, he smiled a little grimly. He would not take Alice home as his wife, no matter how disappointed her family and his mother might be. Alice herself might be angry, but she would not be heartbroken, for he was well aware that though she was prepared to marry him she had not fallen in love with him.

He whistled light-heartedly when he had come to this decision, in spite of the fact that the morning's fitful spring sunshine had given way to raindrops that stung as the wind blew them on his face. Suddenly he saw ahead of him a small figure trudging along with head bent, and as his horse drew abreast of the pedestrian he realised that it was Rose Kingsley. He halted the horse abruptly and held out a hand to Rose as she looked up to see who was passing.

'I met you with Alice Wright, remember? My name is Richard Overton. Mount behind me and I'll take you home!'

She hesitated for only a moment, then scrambled up behind him, clutching the empty basket.

'Thank you again! Our cottage is on this road, about a mile ahead.'

The horse, a sturdy animal used to farm work, carried his double burden easily.

'I see you sold your eggs,' Richard commented.

There was a little chuckle behind him.

'If it hadn't been for your quickness there would have been none to sell! As it was, I managed to keep them safe till I sold them, fortunately.'

'Fortunately?'

'Mother is letting me keep the egg

money until I've saved enough to buy a length of cloth to make myself a new gown,' she informed him. 'What with the rate I'm growing and the way I've got splashed with mud today, the sooner I can afford that the better.'

He felt a passing pity for this young girl who faced her poverty so cheerfully, but a small cottage came in sight before any more was said. It was a low, one-storey building which could not contain more than two rooms. A woman was standing anxiously in the doorway, staring along the road. Rose waved to her as they neared the cottage.

'It's all right, Mother, I'm back! I've been rescued by a knight on a charger.'

As they reached the gate, she slid gracefully from the horse's back. Her mother, a thin woman with a lined face, came out to thank the rescuer effusively.

'You have been very kind, sir. This rain would have soaked my daughter soon. Of course, when my husband was alive and we had our own farm this would not have happened. He would have taken us to the market in our own cart, but those days are gone now, of course!'

She was obviously ready to continue in this way for some time, mixing her thanks with hints about her former standing in life. Anxious to get home and out of the rain, Richard murmured gently that he was glad to have been able to help, and gathered up the reins. As he rode away, he glanced back and saw Rose waving from the cottage door, a mischievous smile on her face. He cheerfully returned the wave.

Mistress Kingsley shut the door and drew Rose close to the fire, hastily rubbing her hair and hands dry.

'Who was that rider and where did you meet him?' she asked inquisitively.

'He's called Richard Overton and he saw me walking home about a mile down the road,' her daughter returned. 'I thought I could accept his offer to bring me back because I met him earlier in the market with Alice Wright.'

Her mother's busy hands stilled.

'With Alice Wright! He must be the young farmer she's got her eye on. Mistress Smithson was telling me that they make a big fuss of him whenever he calls.'

Rose brushed aside a wet lock of hair and wrinkled her nose disparagingly.

'He's a fool if he wants to marry Alice. She has an awful temper, and I suspect she tried to trip me and break my eggs in the market.'

Mistress Kingsley looked at her in horror.

'You broke the eggs?'

Rose shook her head.

'Fortunately, Master Overton caught me before I dropped them. I sold them, but not for much. The stall holders all say their own hens are laying well at present.'

She fumbled in a pocket and held out a few coins for her mother's inspection.

'At this rate you won't get a new gown till the autumn,' the older woman commented grimly.

Rose's lips dropped at the corners, but she had long learned the importance of keeping her mother's spirits up.

'It doesn't matter,' she said stoutly. 'I am sure we can let this one out a little further, or put in a gusset.'

Her mother put the money away and shook her head sadly.

'If only your father was still alive!'

Rose shut her ears to her mother's familiar lament and thought of Richard Overton. She had enjoyed coming home behind a tall, broad-shouldered young man with a pleasant smile. He truly would be wasted on Alice Wright!

In fact it was three weeks before Richard returned to Frotesham. The spring season had kept him busy on the farm until the memory of Alice's bad temper had faded while the picture of her pretty face had not. However, her greeting was a little cool.

'I thought you had found somewhere else to pay your visits,' she said a little tartly.

'As a farmer's daughter you should know what a busy time of the year this is,' he reminded her.

'Oh, of course! I remember you said you were busy when you left last time,' she said sarcastically.

'Indeed I was.'

She rounded on him, eyes flashing and voice shrill.

'Not too busy to meet Rose Kingsley and ride with her on your horse! Not too busy to stop at her ruin of a cottage and talk with her mother! Her mother told Mistress Smithson, who could not wait to tell my mother!'

He felt his face redden furiously.

'Mistress Smithson seems to have made more of the incident than it warranted. I picked up the poor girl because she was getting soaked in the rain and I dropped her at her gate. I didn't even dismount!'

Alice Wright saw with dismay that her display of temper was likely to drive him away, and although she was indifferent to him as a person she was very attracted by his good farm. She heaved a sigh and smiled bravely.

'Forgive me! It was just that the thought of you escorting another young woman made me feel so jealous!'

He appeared to respond to this flattery, but inwardly he was deciding that this was definitely his last visit to the Wrights' farm. Once again he left early, and this time Alice did not dare protest.

Richard's homeward path took him past the Kingsleys' cottage. If he had not been so annoyed with Alice, he would probably never have decided to show his independence by knocking to enquire whether Rose had caught a cold as a result of being soaked in the rainstorm. As it was, she opened the door herself, and her frank pleasure at the sight of him was balm after Alice's difficult ways.

'I called to see if you were well,' Richard said, 'but the answer is obviously yes.'

'I am glad to say so,' she responded,

'though my mother is sure that it was due to your kindness in saving me from getting too wet.'

'Is she here?'

Rose came out into the garden and patted the patient horse.

'She is visiting her friend, Mrs Smithson.'

'Oh, Mrs Smithson,' Richard said with feeling, and she looked at him enquiringly.

'I have been in trouble today because of Mrs Smithson. She gave Mistress Wright a rather misleading account of how I helped you.'

Her eyes widened, and then a dimple flashed for a second.

'And that angered Alice, I suppose.'

'It did indeed.'

'She was always a bad-tempered girl at dame school,' Rose said chattily, and then stopped abruptly. 'I'm sorry! I mustn't say such things about your sweetheart.'

'Alice Wright is not my sweetheart,' Richard said with emphasis.

Rose, about to speak again, thought better of it, and Richard decided it was best to change the subject.

'Have you saved enough for your new gown?'

She shook her head forlornly.

'The pedlar came to the village last week. He said he would bring some stuff for a gown next time, if I wanted it, but I don't think we will have saved enough by then.'

An idea came to Richard, and he acted on it impulsively.

'The pedlar's goods are always more expensive than those you can get in town,' he told her, but she laughed at him.

'That is true, but as I cannot go to town that doesn't help me.'

'Perhaps not, but I am going to Chester next week. If you give me your money I will see what I can find. I have bought fabric for my mother's gowns in the past and she had been very satisfied with my choice.'

Rose hesitated, looking at him

doubtfully. After all, this was only the second time they had met. Richard looked back at her, transparently honest and direct, and her suspicions vanished.

'Do you know how much fabric is needed?' she queried in amusement.

'The merchant will know when I describe you.'

Making up her mind, she darted into the cottage and emerged with her savings. It looked a very small heap of coins as she held it out, and she bit her lip ruefully.

'Please, see what there is in Chester, but if there isn't enough money to buy anything I shall understand.'

He took the coins and slipped them into his pocket, smiling confidently at her.

'I shall find you something,' he promised. 'Meanwhile, I have a farm waiting,' and he swung up into the saddle.

Her mother was torn between horror and delight when she came home and found what had happened.

'He came here 'specially to see how you were? He wanted to see you again? But he is practically promised to Alice Wright.'

'Indeed he is not!' said Rose firmly. 'In fact I think he has changed his mind about Alice now he has discovered her temper.'

'But you gave him your money,' Mistress Kingsley wailed. 'That was rash. Suppose he simply keeps it. No one will believe us if we say he was given it.'

'He is an honest man who is simply carrying out an errand for us,' Rose maintained. 'Wait till next week. Surely it is better to get the material for my gown in Chester if we can get it more cheaply. We'll wait.'

But her confidence had faded when twelve days had passed and Richard did not reappear.

'He is busy on the farm. He will come,' she insisted stubbornly.

On the fifteenth day she was busy weeding the small plot of flowers in front of the cottage when she heard the sound of a horse's hooves, and her spirits rose as she saw Richard approaching. She went to meet him with a brilliant smile.

'Did you think I was never coming?' he greeted her.

'Of course not,' she lied firmly, eyeing the package he carried.

He laughed disbelievingly as her mother came to greet him as well.

'Let me show you how I carried out your instructions,' he told them with obvious satisfaction and inside the cottage he carefully undid the package and spread out its contents.

There was fine grey woollen cloth as good as any Alice Wright had ever worn, a parcel of white linen, and even a length of grey silk ribbon. Rose surveyed it all with delight.

'I was lucky,' Richard told them. 'I met a merchant who was anxious to get rid of the last of his stock so I was able to drive a hard bargain.'

Over Rose's head, his eyes blandly

met her mother's look of disbelief. She knew that no merchant would have dreamed of selling such high-quality goods for the small collection of coins that Rose had saved.

'Isn't it beautiful, Mother?' Rose sighed.

Her mother, eyes still held by Richard's, nodded.

2

Rose smoothed the long grey skirts over her slim hips with slightly contemptuous fingers, and couldn't hide her dismay.

'It's dull!' she proclaimed. 'Dull, drab and boring! I hate it!'

Her companion surveyed her carefully, running his fingers through his short fair hair.

'I wouldn't say that,' he ventured cautiously. 'It's a well-made dress, it fits you, and it's a good, hard-wearing fabric.'

With an exasperated sigh, Rose lifted her clenched fists and thumped his broad chest. Unmoved, he looked down on her with amusement till she dropped her hands and turned away in disgust.

'Do you really mean you can't see anything wrong with it?' she demanded.

Richard Overton smiled at her

lovingly, his blue eyes showing their pleasure at the sight she made with her anger bringing fresh colour to her cheeks and sparkle to her brown eyes. Her fair hair was nearly hidden by her neat white linen cap, which was echoed by the wide white collar of her demure dress.

'I think you look beautiful,' he said sincerely.

Rose's anger was temporarily forgotten as she shook her head at him in mock reproach, breaking into a reluctant smile.

'You say that whatever I'm wearing,' she pointed out.

'Because it's true,' he assured her sincerely.

'Don't you think I would look even more beautiful if my dress was made of red velvet and trimmed with lace? Imagine me with wide, wide skirts, and with the neckline just a little lower.'

For a moment he was captured by the picture she described, and then he shook his head and frowned at her.

'You are thinking of the kind of dress grand ladies wore before the Commonwealth and Lord Protector Cromwell got rid of such vanities,' he said sternly. 'Such clothes are not fitting for England today.'

Rose cast him a rebellious look and then bent her head to scowl at the offending gown.

'There are still ladies in England who wear fine clothes.' She hesitated. 'Now the Cromwells have gone, there may be changes in the Commonwealth.'

They were both silent. Even the inhabitants of the sleepy, Cheshire village of Frotesham were aware of the uncertainties and dangers which threatened the peace that the Commonwealth under Oliver Cromwell had brought them after the bloody civil war had devastated the country. But now Oliver Cromwell was dead, his weak son, Richard, had resigned the power he never wanted, and the country waited to see which leader and which party would triumph in the current power struggle.

'I do not think our lives will change much,' Richard said a little heavily. 'And I do not think a red velvet dress would be very suitable for helping your mother with the work about the cottage.'

Her lips tightened but she did not answer. He was right, of course, but that did not make the bitter truth any the more palatable. She would never be a fine lady, and her life would be spent in housewifery and caring for the garden and animals which provided food. Even if she married Richard, which everybody but Alice Wright and his mother seemed to be taking for granted now, the life of a farmer's wife was not an easy one.

He was leaning on a field gate now, his tall, broad-shouldered figure dressed in a serviceable brown coat which had been made with an eye to practicality rather than with any idea of enhancing the wearer's appearance, and his face had resumed its normal, serious expression. There had been little in his life to make him light-hearted. From his earliest years he had toiled on his father's farm.

For some years his father had been away fighting against the Royalists, only to return disabled by a wound which stopped him working on the farm and turned him into an embittered drunkard who was a burden whom his wife and son supported patiently until his death, two years previously. Rose knew that all his efforts were dedicated to making the farm as prosperous as possible, especially now with the aim of being able to make her his wife. She felt guilty for her previous bad temper, and took Richard's arm.

'Don't worry. I'll forget my fancies and be grateful for my new dress, even if it is grey,' she assured him. 'Now, take me back to my mother, or you won't reach home before it gets dark.'

His face lightened, and he placed his strong hand over hers as they walked through the sunlit summer fields till they reached the small cottage which lay in the shadow of Frotesham Hill. At the gate to the neat garden he halted.

'I'll have to make haste home, as I had to leave the horse for work on the farm, so I won't come inside today.'

She gave a mischievous laugh, and saw the colour rise in his cheeks. They were both aware that if he went in to say goodbye to the garrulous Mistress Kingsley, she was perfectly capable of overwhelming him with a torrent of gossip and small talk that would delay his departure for some time.

All the same, Richard Overton hesitated before he set off, still a little disturbed by the restlessness and dissatisfaction Rose had shown earlier, and wanting somehow to console her for all the finery she wanted but would never have. He could understand how Rose felt.

'I tell you that you are beautiful because you are,' he assured her anxiously. 'It is the simple truth.'

She smiled up at him gratefully.

'I know that is what you believe,' she said softly, 'and it makes me happy.'

He breathed a relieved sigh, picked up her hand, kissed it, and then turned and strode away, a six-mile walk before him. Rose lingered by the gate, watching him until he was lost to sight. In the past two months he had transformed her life and her future prospects. If she married him, he would cherish her and do his best to provide for her, important matters for a girl with no dowry and no menfolk to look after her. He would also help her mother as well, and at this thought, Rose left the sunlight for the dark interior of the little cottage.

'Where's Richard?' were her mother's first words as she saw her daughter enter alone.

'He sent you his regards, but didn't have time to come in to speak to you, Mother.'

'No time to take his leave of me? He had plenty of time to spend with you, I noticed. It was different when your

27

father was alive. Richard Overton would have behaved more respectfully to me then. Your father's clumsiness ruined my life.'

As usual, Rose forbore to point out that the fall from a ladder which had killed her father had dramatically changed her own life as well. Before then his wife and daughter had lived in comfort with servants to help in the house and dairy. After his death the two women had been fortunate to have been allowed to take over the two-room cottage with its small patch of land.

Mistress Kingsley had never got over the fall in status, painfully aware of any slight, real or imagined. Her daughter regretted past comforts but had adjusted with the resilience of youth. Perhaps it was only natural that Mistress Kingsley had grown so sour, aware that her circumstances were unlikely to change for the better so late in life. It was Rose's youth that gave her optimism, the belief that the future would be brighter.

'Richard Overton may own his farm, unlike my poor husband, but he should not ignore me,' her mother continued resentfully.

'Richard is grateful, Mother, and he does not ignore you. In fact, as I was going to tell you, he and his mother have invited us both to go to Overton Farm next Sunday.'

Her mother's eyes widened, but then her voice grew shrill.

'Am I supposed to be grateful to be given a meal by that woman? She's so certain that she's right about everything. She will be unbearably rude to us and treat us like beggars. You know how disappointed she is that her precious son is not going to marry Alice Wright. I'd rather stay here and go hungry!'

'I'll go and feed the hens,' Rose said hurriedly, escaping outside.

On Sunday, Richard had arranged with a carter that they should bring Rose and her mother to Overton Farm, and in spite of her protestations to Rose, Mistress Kingsley mounted the cart without delay, with a fierce sparkle in her eye as if she were preparing to go into battle. At Overton Farm, Richard's stately mother waited to greet her guests. She kissed Rose's proffered cheek, but her eyes were on the older woman

'Mistress Kingsley, you are welcome.'

'Mistress Overton, how pleasant to see you again!'

The greetings were part of a ritual as the two women surveyed each other and their opponent's child, looking for some fault. This time Mistress Overton struck first.

'Rose is looking well. Richard told me she had a new gown. I know it must have been hard for you to afford it, but then we mothers will always scrimp and save to make sure our children look well, no matter what old clothes we wear.'

She smoothed her respectable gown complacently. Conscious of the fact that her own gown was well past its best, Mistress Kingsley forced a smile.

'Indeed, that is true, and Rose repays dressing well. After all, a fine gown can do little for someone who has lost her figure.'

And she looked pointedly at Mistress Overton's plump form. And so battle was joined, and sharp tongues were searching for even more cutting remarks as Rose and Richard stole away for a few quiet minutes together.

'Why must they argue?' Rose asked helplessly.

'Because they enjoy it,' Richard replied. 'Mother gets bored when there's no problem to tackle, and I believe she has been looking forward to a day of trading insults with your mother.'

Rose pursed her lips thoughtfully.

'You may be right. Mother always seems to be happier and have more energy after a good argument with someone like your mother. At least it makes her forget the past.'

She slipped her hand through his arm.

'Let's forget them for a bit. What was the news at the Chester market this week? Who is our ruler now?'

His broad shoulders shrugged.

'Who knows? Cromwell's old commanders are scheming against each other now, each conspiring to seize power. While they are watching each other, the Royalists are seeing a chance to rise again.'

She looked at him disbelievingly.

'Surely the Royalists don't think they can restart the war. Charles is in exile, living on the French King's charity, and their war leaders are dead or proved incompetent.'

'England has had kings for a lot longer than it has had a Commonwealth. If the new scheme of things doesn't work, people may want a return to the old ways.'

But politics was only a series of rumours, and all the majority of the people could do was hope for a peaceful solution which would let the country prosper under a lawful government, and Richard and Rose soon dropped the subject in favour of more local affairs.

They returned to the farmhouse to find Mistress Overton busy loading the table with dishes, and when they sat down to their dinner she pressed the good food upon them.

'It gives me great pleasure to be able to sit at my own table and offer my guests a good dinner,' she announced.

'Enjoy it while you can,' Mistress Kingsley responded tartly. 'After all, when Richard marries it will be his wife who presides in your place.'

Mistress Overton grew agitated and her knife clattered on her plate.

'Richard is only twenty-five, far too young to think of marriage. He's a sensible young man who will wait until he finds a girl with a good dowry, someone who will bring land or money to the match, like Alice Wright.'

The meal was finished in near silence, and soon after, Richard got the horse and cart ready for the return journey. Mistress Kingsley steadily refused Mistress Overton's offer of a bed for the night, insisting that she could only sleep in her own home.

When they reached Frotesham, Richard snatched a word with Rose.

'Don't take any notice of what Mother said at dinner,' he pleaded. 'She loves you like a daughter.'

'And she would much rather I were her daughter than her son's wife,' Rose commented wryly then she smiled at Richard's downcast expression.

'Don't worry. My mother provoked her, and they are both probably ashamed of themselves now.'

She stood on tip-toe and kissed his cheek.

'I'll forgive your mother if you'll forgive me.'

He cheered up amazingly at this small sign of affection and left promising to bring her some treat from the market next time he went. She waved him goodbye, not expecting to see him for a good few days as the animals and growing crops demanded his care.

But he was hammering at their door within a week, the sweat-darkened coat of his horse showing how hard he had ridden it. The mere sight of him put them into a state of alarm.

'There's danger afoot!' he told them. 'Royalists have risen in the county, and some say they have even entered Chester itself. You must pack what you can carry and come to the farm. My labourers are there and we can protect you.'

White-faced, Rose was prepared to obey him, but her mother stood obstinately still.

'I've lost one home,' she said roundly. 'What's in this cottage is all I have, and I'm not leaving it to be plundered or destroyed by any vagabonds.'

'But you are both in danger if the fighting spreads. Two women on their own will be helpless.'

'I have my husband's musket, and I can use it if need be. If we do hear that troops are on the way we'll go to stay with the Smithsons. They have a well-built house and can withstand an attack as well as Overton Farm.'

Richard's arguments could not move her and Rose would not leave her mother. Richard reluctantly rode back alone.

'I'd rather face a troop of Royalists than spend a night under the same roof as his mother. That woman and I would be at each other's throats,' Mistress Kingsley said with satisfaction.

No troops of Royalist or Parliament soldiers thundered through their quiet lanes in the following days, in spite of rumours. One evening, Rose opened the door to a timid knock, while Mistress Kingsley stood near with musket ready, and found two tired, hungry Royalist fugitives who craved only a little food before they made their way back home. Mistress Kingsley decided to exchange the food for news, for there was obviously nothing to fear from these two.

'We did enter Chester,' one said with

a flicker of military pride, 'but the castle was held against us. Then our leaders started bickering among themselves as usual and we were no match for the trained troops who came against us.'

'Are Parliament's troops likely to be hunting you?' Rose said with some anxiety, but the lad shook his head.

'They're only interested in catching the gentlefolk who led us, not the poor infantry.'

John Lambert, Cromwell's former major-general, crushed that August rising in Cheshire, and was soon to go on to lead his troops into London. Life in the Cheshire villages returned to its quiet routine. There was a spate of petty crimes, and Mistress Kingsley had to bewail the disappearance of two of her best hens.

The less law-abiding element seemed to feel that if no one was sure who was running the country, the authority by which magistrates and constables maintained the law of the land was also in doubt.

In compensation, it was a good harvest that year, and Richard Overton surveyed the rich countryside with satisfaction.

'If we can gather in the harvest safely, I shall make a tidy profit,' he told Rose one day. 'The farm has recovered from the bad years.'

The months passed, and it was on Christmas Day that Richard asked Rose to marry him.

'I can support a wife now. There is no reason why we should not marry in the next few weeks.'

The words gave her a shock. She had accepted that one day she would marry him, but she was eighteen years old and that one day had been a very vague date in the future.

'What do you say?' he said eagerly.

She laughed uneasily, uncertain what to say now that he was pressing for a decision.

'But we're not even formally betrothed yet,' she prevaricated. 'And what would your mother say at such a rushed wedding?'

'What does a betrothal matter?' he said impatiently. 'As for Mother, no matter what she says, she has accepted that you will be my wife. If we marry now we could have a child by next Christmas.'

Rose nearly panicked. Marriage and then a child! Her youth would be over and all the glorious possibilities of life would narrow down to the same type of narrow existence as her mother's and Mistress Overton's.

'Give me time,' she pleaded. 'Let me think about it.'

'I brought it out too suddenly,' Richard said ruefully. 'Mother always said I was too blunt. I should have led up to it with a bit of flowery language.'

He looked tenderly at Rose.

'But I do love you, and I do want to marry you.'

'Give me time,' she repeated.

'I'll give you a week,' he said.

He was sure that he knew what her answer would be when he came for it, and she knew that for her mother's sake as well as her own she would accept his proposal.

3

Mistress Kingsley wondered why her daughter was so quiet and absent-minded during the next few days. Rose did not want to discuss Richard's proposal with her mother, for she knew the older woman would not be able to understand why she was so hesitant about accepting him.

The week seemed to pass with frightening speed, until the day came when Richard would appear to hear her answer, and Rose knew that it would have to be yes. She told herself how many girls, such as Alice Wright, would have been happy to be in her position, and that she should be happy. At least she would look her best when he came, she decided, putting on her new gown and arranging her hair carefully under her best cap.

Her mother, ignorant of the momentous event that was to take place that day, took herself off early to the Smithsons, their nearest neighbours, a family of tenant-farmers with a daughter near Rose's age. Mrs Smithson had been a gossip companion of Mistress Kingsley long before the farm had been lost, and was always careful to treat her friend with the same respect as she had shown her in the days before she had fallen on hard times.

Rose expected her mother to be gone for the full morning, and was taken by surprise when she burst excitedly into the cottage where Rose was preparing vegetables for their meal.

'Put those down, girl, and go and get that hen I killed and plucked. And bring me a basket. I want something to put the eggs in!'

'What's happened? Is there to be some celebration or are they for someone who is ill?'

'It's nothing like that! Now, move quickly before word spreads!'

'About what?'

Her mother busied herself collecting together a selection of their small store of food even as she replied.

'There are guests at Hawsby Hall, gentry. They arrived last night with virtually no warning and found the house cold and with nothing to eat. They were not best pleased, from what I hear from the Smithsons. If we can get there soon they will be grateful for what we can offer and should pay well.'

All became clear. Frotesham and much of the surrounding area belonged to the Earl of Dunsdale, who had managed to retain most of his vast estates during and after the Civil War. He owned the house and park of Hawsby Hall, an ancient building which had once been the manor house of the area, but only the oldest inhabitant could remember him visiting these possessions, as he much preferred his estates in the Yorkshire Dales.

The great house had stayed empty for many years except for the elderly

43

steward, Michael Johnson, who occupied a couple of rooms and neglected
the rest. The unexpected arrival of
visitors expecting to find a house and
welcome fit for the nobility must have
come as a considerable shock to him.

Mistress Kingsley and Rose, both
carrying baskets covered with white
cloth, arrived at the hall to find that the
news had apparently spread already. By
the stables, farmers were offering hay
for the horses, and large joints of meat
were being lifted off carts.

'Let's go round to the side door,'
Mistress Kingsley whispered. 'We can
find our way to the kitchen from there.'

Unobtrusively, they slipped away
from the crowd and made their way
into the house and along the passages
until they reached the kitchen, where
they found a real frenzy of activity. A
round, red-faced woman was trying to
impose order, but broke off when she
saw the newcomers.

'Mistress Kingsley! Rose! At least if
you have brought us something I can be

sure it is worth having.'

'A good fat hen and two dozen fresh eggs,' Mistress Kingsley told her, 'but we've brought them to sell, not as gifts.'

'That's understood. Tell the man over there what you've brought, and then come back to me. I know you've got a good light hand with pastry.'

It became clear that Michael Johnson had tried to deal with the emergency by recruiting all the help he could find and then relying on the dominant characters to take charge and organise matters.

'Who are these important visitors, Susan? We seem to be preparing food for an army!' Rose asked the young girl with whom she began peeling apples.

Susan Smithson giggled light-heartedly.

'There is only one member of the gentry, but she seems to have brought dozens of servants!'

'One woman? Who is she?'

'It's Lady Stretton, Lady Amanda Stretton. Her husband is cousin to the earl, and that is why she has been allowed to come here to break her journey. Her husband went to France with young Charles Stuart, he who claims to be King of England, after the defeat at Worcester, and she stayed in this country to look after his property. Now she's on her way to London.'

'London!'

Both girls looked at each other, awed by the mere idea of the great city which they would never see.

'Are those things ready yet?' an exasperated call came, and they bent themselves over their work again.

Eventually the apples and vegetables were prepared and delivered to the cook, who seemed to be making progress in preparing a suitable meal for one lady and her servants. There appeared to be no further demands for the girls' services, and they stood in the kitchen rather at a loss until Susan gave a sudden gasp and pulled at Rose's sleeve.

'I've had an idea! Why don't we try and see Lady Stretton? There are so many strangers in the house that no one will notice us.'

Rose looked round swiftly, and saw her mother was fully engaged as a pastry-cook.

'Quickly then, before they find us more work!' and she pushed the other girl ahead of her out of the kitchen.

Susan had been right when she said that no one would notice them making their way through the house, and there was no difficulty in locating Lady Stretton. Everybody's attention was focused in the direction of one room, and as the girls neared it they could hear a silvery voice raised in obvious displeasure. Edging their way through the crowd in the doorway, they stared at the scene before them.

Michael Johnson, the earl's steward, who had held power for so many years over the tenants of the estate, stood with head hanging guiltily before a dark-haired woman in her thirties who was making her displeasure very clear.

'My kinsman, the earl, your master,

assured me that I would be greeted as became my rank and given suitable accommodation. Instead, I arrive to find cold, bare, dirty rooms, and no food ready for myself or my servants.'

Michael Johnson could be heard muttering that her messenger had arrived only minutes before she had, but Lady Stretton swept on as if he had not spoken.

'I have spent a miserable night in damp sheets. This morning I can scarcely breathe because of the smoky fires. There was no hot water for my toilette, and all I was offered to break my fast was coarse country bread and stale cheese!'

'Michael Johnson is in trouble for sure,' Susan muttered, but Rose did not hear her.

Her rapt attention was held by the figure of Lady Stretton. Like Rose, she wore a grey gown, but hers was of velvet, with a light pearly sheen that could never be regarded as dull or serviceable. Her collar was of fine lace, her skirts full and sweeping. For the first time Rose saw in the flesh the kind of fine lady she had long dreamed about, and the reality was far better than the vision.

Oblivious of her audience, the angry noblewoman swept on.

'My coachman tells me the stables were not fit for our horses, and that only now is hay arriving for them. My maid was too ill to travel with us, and you have no housekeeper. I dressed myself as well as I could this morning, but I need help. Who is to get my clothes ready and help me with my hair and toilette?'

No one was more surprised than Rose when she heard her voice say, 'I can do that, your ladyship.'

Lady Stretton's head snapped round toward the door, and the other servants hurriedly shuffled aside, leaving Rose to face the lady. She curtsied carefully and advanced a little, head up under the noblewoman's scrutiny.

'My mother says I have a deft hand

with clothes, and I can arrange hair neatly.'

Biting her lip consideringly, Lady Stretton examined Rose at length, and finally, grudgingly, seemed to find her acceptable.

'I can see you've turned yourself out reasonably well at least, and it looks as if I have no other choice for now. Well, come to my bedchamber, and I'll see if you are speaking the truth.'

The doorway emptied like magic as the lady swept through it followed by Rose, who snatched a second to ask Susan Smithson to tell her mother what was happening. Her friend disappeared, agog with the news, and Rose felt very alone as she followed Lady Stretton. The bedchamber seemed a very handsome room to Rose in contrast to the rustic housing she had always known, though it was clear that a good housekeeper would not have approved of the lack of polish or sweet herbs, and the bed hangings were sadly faded.

Under Lady Stretton's supervision,

Rose extracted clothes and linen from chests on the floor and spread them out on the bed. Then Lady Stretton sat down, pulled off her cap, and instructed Rose to arrange her hair afresh.

'I made a sad tangle of it this morning,' she frowned, 'and I will not go through the day with it in such a mess.'

Rose's hands were quick and efficient, and the soft dark hair was soon tidy and re-covered with the dainty cap. Her ladyship surveyed herself closely in a looking-glass and pronounced herself satisfied.

'Almost as good as my maid would have done it,' she observed, but Rose hardly heard the words of praise.

Looking-glasses were rare and prized objects and she was trying to sneak a look at her own reflection. Amused, Lady Stretton studied the girl, and a spark of interest came into her vivid blue eyes.

'I forgot to ask your name, girl.'

'Rose Kingsley, your ladyship,' Rose

51

replied and bobbed another curtsey.

'A pretty name for a pretty girl. Are you a farmer's daughter?'

'I was, but Father died. Now my mother and I live in a cottage near here.'

'Just the two of you? Life must be hard. No brother, or menfolk? Perhaps you have a sweetheart? Are you promised to anyone?'

'No, ma'am,' Rose said briefly, while very conscious of the fact that in a few hours Richard would call to receive her answer and the situation would change completely.

While Rose carried out a few minor tasks according to Lady Stretton's instructions, the older woman watched her carefully. Finally she smiled, as if a decision had been made.

'Come here, Rose.'

Rose advanced obediently, expecting some coins as a reward for her work, but Lady Stretton's white hands were empty.

'Are you happy with your life here in

your cottage?' she enquired.

Rose hesitated, frowned. It was not a matter she had considered much. After all, what was the point if there was no alternative? Finally she shook her head slowly.

'I can't say I am really happy. It is very dull and rather hard.'

'While London is very exciting. Would you like to see London?'

Rose nodded wistfully.

'I would love to, but I doubt if I ever shall.'

Lady Stretton's voice was as smooth and soft as silk.

'I could take you there.'

Rose's face lit up with sudden hope and she waited eagerly for the woman to continue.

'As you heard me say, my maid is ill and could not travel with me, and I do not expect her to follow me to London for some time. Now you obviously have the talent to be an excellent lady's maid. Will you come with me when I leave tomorrow?'

A chance to go to London! Rose's instinct was to accept the offer instantly, but she was forced to remember the one great obstacle. Richard would soon be at the cottage demanding her answer, and then she would be committed to staying in Cheshire, for ever. Lady Stretton saw the struggle of emotions on her face and spoke a little impatiently.

'Is there any reason why you should not come with me? Surely your mother will see it as a chance for you to learn new skills which you can use to good effect when you return. Is there anything which you cannot postpone for a few months?'

Nothing, was the answer. Richard had not expected to be able to afford to marry her so soon, so why shouldn't they wait a while? She could see London and come back with her wages as a small dowry with which to start life as a farmer's wife. The chance to see London would never come again.

'There is nothing to keep me here,

your ladyship. I will come to London with you,' she said firmly.

Her ladyship smiled with satisfaction.

'Then go and tell your mother that we are leaving tomorrow. I can manage to get myself to bed tonight, but I shall expect you to be here early ready to help me and ready to leave before the day is very old.'

Mistress Kingsley was gone when Rose went back to the kitchen with her news. She'd left some time ago to walk home with Susan Smithson, the cook told her. Gathering up her skirts, Rose ran along the lanes, desperate to tell her mother the news and get her on her side before Richard arrived. But when she came in sight of the cottage she stopped abruptly, for Richard's horse was cropping steadily at the grassy verge.

Richard was listening to Mistress Kingsley's account of Lady Stretton's sudden descent on Hawsby Hall, chuckling with her at Michael Johnson's discomfiture, when Rose hurried in with her head up and a bright smile on her lips. She saw the glad look in his eyes and was guiltily aware that he thought the smile was to welcome him, but instead she ignored him and danced up to her mother.

'Guess what I have to tell you! The best news in the world! Lady Stretton is to take me with her to London as her lady's maid.'

Her mother's mouth fell open with surprise before she gave an excited cry and embraced her daughter.

'London? As her ladyship's maid? Oh, the sights you'll see and the clothes she'll give you!'

'Rose!'

It was one quiet, despairing word from Richard. She turned to him, refusing to allow her smile to fade at the sight of his stricken face.

'Isn't it marvellous, Richard? I'll only be away a few months till her maid rejoins her, so it won't matter much for us.'

He stood upright, his face stern, and

gestured towards the door.

'May I have a word with you in private?'

'If you wish,' she said, her deliberate cheerfulness beginning to fade.

They walked a few yards and then turned to face each other. Rose waited to see what he would say.

'Rose,' he began earnestly, 'you know I came here today for your answer to my proposal. I want us to marry before summer. How can you think of going to London?'

She shrugged with affected casualness.

'Before summer, in the autumn, what does it matter? As I said, I shall only be away a few months, and we can get married when I return. I'll bring my wages back with me, too!'

He gestured impatiently.

'Do you really think I care about a few pounds? The fact is, Rose, that given the choice between marrying me and going to London you have chosen London.'

She was stubbornly silent, but the pain she saw in his face almost made her throw her arms about him and promise to stay. But the vision of London kept her where she was.

'I always knew I loved you more than you loved me,' he said heavily, 'but I told myself that you did care for me. Now I know I was deluding myself. You are just like Alice Wright. I was your only chance to escape from poverty, but now you have the opportunity to travel the land and see the city, live in a great house and watch the gentlefolk, and you are seizing that chance without a moment's hesitation. If you cared for me at all, our marriage and life with me would have come before everything.'

He waited for her to speak, but her lips were pressed shut. He did not know that she felt that if she tried to speak she would burst into tears. She tried to combat her feeling of guilt with anger that he should dare to speak to her so.

He sighed resignedly.

'Give my regards to your mother,' he

told her, mounting his horse. 'As for you, Rose, you will always have my love, no matter how little you value it,' and with that he rode away without a backward glance.

4

Rose went slowly back to the cottage to face her mother's torrent of questions. Mistress Kingsley was thrilled at the sudden news, as animated and talkative as though she were the person about to undertake the grand adventure and not her daughter. She was taken aback, however, when she learned how soon Rose must leave.

'Tomorrow? Early? But how can you be ready by morning?'

'I've little enough to take, Mother. We can pack my clothes and other necessities in half-an-hour.'

Her mother sank into a chair.

'But that means you'll be gone before I've thought of half the things I want to say to you. And you won't have time to say goodbye to your friends. What about Richard?'

'I've said goodbye to him.'

Mistress Kingsley caught the sad note in her voice.

'He looked so happy today when he was waiting for you. Why did he hurry away? I would have thought that he would have wanted to spend these last few hours with you.'

Rose shocked herself for the second time that day by sitting down and bursting into tears. Her mother's arms were round her instantly.

'What's the matter, my love? Did you quarrel with Richard?'

'Last week he asked me to marry him soon and he looked happy when he came today because he expected me to say that I would. Instead I told him that I was going to London. Now he thinks I don't love him.'

Her mother grew still, cautiously enquiring after a while, 'And do you?'

Rose turned and clung to her mother like a child.

'I don't know. At times I think I do, but I don't want to marry him or anyone yet. I'm too young and if I have the chance to see something of life outside this village before I settle down then I want to take the opportunity.'

Her mother stroked her hair, making no comment, until Rose took a shuddering sigh, dried her eyes, and said she must start to get ready for the morning. The two worked quickly together, and soon a small bundle of belongings had been assembled. Rose looked at it.

'Well, it doesn't seem much to start a new life with, but it's all I've got. Now I'd better get what sleep I can.'

But both of them lay sleepless for most of that night, and they had risen and dressed even before the grey dawn showed in the east, and they broke their fast in virtual silence. As they cleared away the small meal, Mistress Kingsley turned to her daughter with sudden resolution.

'Rose, it's not too late to change your mind.'

Rose was putting on a brave face.

'Why should I do that? As I told

Richard, I shall only be gone for a few months, then it will be as if I had never left.'

'You think he will wait for you, then?' Rose stared at her mother in amazement.

'Of course he will! He said some bitter things yesterday because he was disappointed that I want to postpone our marriage, but he loves me. It was the last thing he said.'

'Love can die, especially when one partner chooses to leave the other. When you are gone he will remember that you preferred London to marrying him. He may find someone eager to comfort him.'

'You mean Alice Wright? He would never go back to her!'

'Perhaps not, but there are others who see him as a good man who would make a good husband. I don't want you to lose him.'

Rose tossed her head impatiently.

'Perhaps I'll find someone better in London.'

'It would be difficult. Do you remember how he took the egg money and bought the stuff for your new gown in Chester?'

'Of course.'

'And did you ever realise that your little store of money would not even have paid for the linen for the collar and cap? He paid for the stuff out of his own pocket, as a kindness to a young girl who needed a new dress.'

Rose stood still with an angry sparkle in her eyes.

'So he was being generous to a poor girl, was he? Well, he didn't buy me along with the gown. When I come back from London I will marry him if he is waiting for me. If he finds someone else in the meantime, so be it.'

She would not discuss the matter further, talking busily of messages to be given her friends and how she would find some way of letting her mother know how she was getting on in London.

When light filled the sky, she picked

up her bundle and the two women set out for Hawsby Hall. While her mother stayed in the kitchen talking to the cook, Rose went to Lady Stretton's bedchamber. She found her up, wrapped in a loose robe, and waiting for her ministrations. After my lady had washed and had been helped to dress and then have her hair arranged, she sat in a chair and directed Rose how to pack, revealing a sharp eye when a garment was about to be placed carelessly in a trunk. The inexperienced girl was amazed at the amount that my lady had required for the two-night stay.

She did not realise how quickly the time was passing until Lady Stretton summoned menservants to carry her luggage to the coach, and Rose was suddenly aware that soon she, too, would be climbing into a coach and leaving Frotesham. Her courage nearly failed her, and she felt ready to run from the room and from the house back to the familiar cottage. But Lady

Stretton was waiting impatiently for a fine cloak to be wrapped around her shoulders, and then she beckoned Rose to follow her.

Outside Rose found three coaches waiting. One was for Lady Stretton, the second was for the servants, including Rose, and the third would lumber along with the luggage. Rose clung for a moment to her mother who was waiting by the coaches, and then climbed into the coach where four yawning servants reluctantly shuffled sufficiently to give her space to sit.

In spite of the early hour, a number of people had assembled to see the departure of the great lady and her entourage, some of them aware that she would be taking a local girl with her. As the horses were urged into action by the coachmen's whips and the travelling carriages lurched forward, Rose gave a sudden gasp and stared out of the window.

Richard Overton was standing a little apart from the other onlookers, in the shadow of a great oak. For a second they seemed to look into each other's eyes. Then Rose saw another figure behind Richard. Alice Wright was wasting no time. Rose sank back, suddenly convinced that she was making a dreadful mistake. For some time she sat silently, deep in her own thoughts, while the other occupants of the coach, three men and a woman, snatched a little more sleep.

Finally, natural curiosity roused Rose to look at her companions, and she realised that the middle-aged woman was surveying her with equal interest.

'So, you are the girl who has suddenly become the lady's maid,' the woman commented with a sniff.

'Well, when Lady Stretton's maid fell ill she needed a replacement, and she seemed to find me suitable.'

The woman laughed scornfully.

'Fell ill? Martha Jones walked out when she could not bear Lady Stretton's whims and tantrums any longer, as other maids have done before her. At least she was near her home. Perhaps Lady Stretton is counting on the fact that if you want to escape from her in London you will have nowhere to go.'

Rose felt even worse.

'Perhaps I will be able to please Lady Stretton. You are still in her service, anyway.'

'Not me! I belong to the Earl of Dunsdale's household, and he asked her to take me to London so that I can visit my sister. After all, it was a small favour in return for the way she's lived off him for the last six months.'

'I thought Lady Stretton had been staying on her husband's estate.'

The men were awake and listening by now, and were amused by this.

'Lady Stretton came north last year to sell what remained of her husband's lands, but after that she came to visit the earl without waiting to be invited and has stayed in his castle ever since, until he almost had to tell her to go.'

'The recent Royalist uprisings decided her to return to London in the end,' another man put in. 'She says that she will be safer there, but I doubt if that is her real reason. After all, there are few places more secure than the Earl of Dunsdale's castle.'

Rose was puzzled.

'But if Lord Stretton no longer owns land in England, why doesn't Lady Stretton follow him to France?'

It was clear that the other four could hardly believe her naïveté.

'Even in Cheshire you must know that husbands and wives sometimes prefer to live apart,' the first man jeered.

The woman was shaking her head sadly.

'Lord and Lady Stretton saw little of each other for years before he went to France. They fought like cat and dog when they did meet, both of them wanting what little money there was for themselves.'

'But Lady Stretton is a great lady!' Rose remonstrated.

'Great ladies do not always pay their

bills,' she was told.

The coaches lumbered on, stopping briefly at an inn for an hour, when a meal of bread and meat and ale was quickly consumed by the servants while Lady Stretton dined in a private room. Then the slow journey continued.

The night was spent as guests at some manor house whose owners accommodated Lady Stretton and her servants adequately but without much warmth. When Rose was summoned to help Lady Stretton prepare for bed she found her in high dudgeon.

'I was informed that I was too tired to join the family, so my supper would be served in my room,' she told Rose. 'Tired, indeed! The truth is that Sir Peter's wife does not want to give him the opportunity to compare the plain little dumpling he married with a woman of real birth and breeding!'

She looked at Rose suspiciously.

'You are very quiet and dull-looking this evening.'

Rose forced a smile.

'I was too excited to sleep last night, and it has been a long day.'

That was true, of course, but although she felt exhausted she still found it difficult to sleep. Rose shared a bed with the woman from the coach, and listened miserably to her snores for some hours.

'I should have stayed in Frotesham,' she told herself. 'I wish I was back with my mother in the cottage, planning my wedding to Richard.'

The next few days passed in much the same fashion. Each night was spent as the guests at yet another house, and from talk in the servants' hall Rose soon discovered that Lady Stretton was tolerated as a guest rather than welcomed.

'Lord Garsdon could hardly shut the door on her when she requested shelter at short notice,' one housekeeper said grumpily. 'We know what she is like from other visits, however. She'll demand the best and then not leave a penny as a reward for the servants. At least we've learned to make sure that she doesn't accidentally pack any small pieces of plate when she goes.'

At the beginning of the journey this would have made Rose shrink with embarrassment and wish herself back in Cheshire, but she was growing used to such remarks. What did it matter what people thought of Lady Stretton? She was just the means Rose was using to fulfil her own dreams of seeing London.

Finally, just when life seemed to have become a never-ending journey, they reached London. Rose woke from an uneasy doze late one afternoon to find the coaches driving through busy streets, the coachmen cursing carts and pedestrians who blocked their progress. The woman who had travelled with her shook her fully awake.

'We'll be at Stretton Place soon, and then I'll be off to my sister's as soon as I've got my belongings.'

Rose looked at her with sudden desolation.

'I'll miss you,' she blurted out.

The woman laughed comfortably.

'That's because you've been missing your mother and I've taken her place,' she pointed out. 'Well, from today you are on your own. You're a sensible lass, though you are young, so look after yourself.'

She leaned over to speak confidentially in the girl's ear.

'I know it's a great adventure to come to London, but if I were you I'd take the first chance that offers to go back to Cheshire and that sweetheart you've told me about.'

Within an hour, the coaches had reached Stretton Place and the woman was gone, leaving Rose feeling desolate and friendless. She found herself in a great house with a warren of rooms and without a friend in the world. This did not last long, of course. Her young spirits revived when she found herself welcomed as a newcomer in the servants' hall by retainers who greeted her as a novelty.

'So you are a country girl from

Cheshire. Do you think you'll survive in London?' one man demanded.

'Could you survive for a week in Cheshire?' she shot back, and the servants applauded her spirit.

In addition, now she was back in her own home, Lady Stretton was showing unexpected regard and care for her new maid.

'Rose must have her own room,' she instructed the housekeeper.

Rose, for the first time in her life, found herself the sole occupant of a chamber not far from those which the Stretton family themselves would use. Lady Stretton told her that this was for the sake of convenience. Her personal maid should be accommodated as near her as possible.

For the first few days in London, Rose was dazzled by the sheer size and activity of the city. She could quickly lose herself in the narrow streets, only to find herself unexpectedly caught up in some crowded market with all kinds of unfamiliar luxuries being offered for her delight. The great houses of the nobility towered above the lesser dwellings. Some stood empty, their owners fled to the safety of France with the so-called King Charles the Second, but others still housed gentlefolk who supported the Commonwealth or were reluctant to abandon their homes, while the rest had passed to new masters.

To Rose, their retinues of servants seemed as numerous as the population of a village, with the strict hierarchy of rank from steward or butler down to kitchen maid mimicking the social order of the world outside. Other aspects of her new life were not so pleasing. London was a great city, but after a life in quiet Cheshire, she found it difficult to tolerate the sheer noise and bustle of the streets, and after the fresh air of the countryside, the fetid smells of the rubbish heaps and open sewers that served London made her feel sick.

'How can you bear to live here?' she wailed to one of the other servants.

Peter, a footman, smiled ruefully back at her.

'We are used to it. It is all we have known.'

She felt Peter was the only real friend she had made in London. At thirty, he was resigned to a life in the service of some great family. His original hope had been to be a lawyer, but his father had been fined heavily after supporting Charles I in the Civil War, and his son had been forced to find employment where he could.

Rose sometimes felt a little guilty about Peter. She regarded him as a friend and helper, but she was uneasily aware that by seeking out his company, she might be arousing feelings other than friendship. Could he replace Richard?

She dismissed the idea as soon as it arose, surprising herself by her realisation that Richard was the standard by which she judged every other man, and that no other man so far could compare with him. Anyway, so far, Peter seemed indifferent to her charms and those of every other woman in the household. When she delicately raised this matter with one of the housemaids, the girl looked at her scornfully.

'He thinks himself too good for the likes of us. He thought his betters were going to make him a gentleman at one time. Well, he's learned his lesson. Now he's glad to be a footman.'

She said nothing more, and Rose did not question her. Peter's past was not her concern. Other things did worry her, however. At first she was overawed by the spacious oak-panelled rooms of Stretton Place, with walls hung with elaborate tapestries and family portraits gazing down at her as she hurried past, but Rose had been raised by a keen housekeeper and could not help noticing that the house was not well maintained.

Some of the furniture needed repair, and in daylight the tapestries showed wear that a careful needlewoman could have repaired. But nobody bothered about these matters. Lady Stretton dined well, but her servants lived on a poor diet of inferior food or stole the food meant for their betters. Although Lady Stretton was a frequent guest at other houses, she herself rarely entertained. Whatever money she had acquired from the sale of her husband's northern estates was certainly not being spent on Stretton Place.

Rose grew more homesick as her boredom increased. She missed the comparative freedom of her former life in the green fields. Here in London she felt almost a prisoner in the great house. Lady Stretton was a demanding employer who expected Rose to be available to tend to her appearance or her wardrobe frequently each day. When she did have some free time she was warned that it was often dangerous out alone in the streets.

One evening found her hurrying up to Lady Stretton's room. Her ladyship had torn some lace and wanted it mended, so Rose had decided to occupy herself with the work that evening. She opened the door of the room, thinking Lady Stretton had gone out. For a second she stood appalled at what she saw, then hurriedly closed the door as silently as possible. Turning away, her cheeks blazing scarlet, she found Peter had climbed the stairway behind her and was now looking at her enquiringly.

'Has something upset you? Is Lady Stretton in a temper?'

'No, nothing like that. I thought the room would be empty, but Lady Stretton was there!'

'And not alone, I presume.'

She nodded miserably and Peter beckoned her away from the door and farther along the landing.

'Lady Stretton is there with a man! They were embracing!'

She faltered to a stop with embarrassment, but Peter showed no sign of shock.

'He is not the first man to have found his way up the back stairs to Lady

Stretton's room. Indeed, for a few weeks I myself found favour with her ladyship. I still remembered enough from my gentle education to please her. Then she decided that she could not afford a liaison with someone without money, but graciously allowed me to stay on as footman. A prouder man would have left her house, but I am weak, Rose. I wanted to eat. Go home to Cheshire, Rose. London can only harm you. Go home before it is too late.'

5

This incident did make some matters clearer to Rose, such as the servants' contempt for their mistress. At first she had been shocked by the indifferent attitude of the other servants. They skimped their work or neglected it altogether, and often spoke disrespectfully of Lady Stretton.

One morning she saw John Stubbs, a footman, casually take a bottle of brandy and tuck it into his pocket. When he looked up and saw Rose staring at him, he lifted an eyebrow interrogatively.

'And what's troubling you?'

'That brandy is Lady Stretton's,' she said accusingly. 'You're stealing it!'

He laughed, obviously untroubled by her accusation.

'I'm not stealing it,' he said with rough humour. 'I'm taking it in place of my wages, which haven't been paid for some time. Have you been paid yet, my little country girl? Do you even know how much you're supposed to be getting?'

When she stood speechless, the colour rising in her cheeks, he nodded sagely.

'I thought so. You'll learn to take what you can here, my girl.'

With that, he swung out of the room, whistling, leaving Rose deeply troubled. London was not what she expected and she had decided to leave Stretton Place and return to Cheshire as soon as she could, but she would need money for the journey. It was true that on the few occasions she had dared to raise the subject of her wages, Lady Stretton had not given her an answer, apparently always distracted by some passing thought or occurrence. However, she had often given Rose occasional coins, or a castoff garment, but that was not the same as a definite, agreed sum, no matter how small.

Rose's purse was virtually empty.

Other incidents made her aware that money might be even scarcer than it first appeared to be in the Stretton household. There was little sign of the family silver that most noble families had accumulated over the years, and more than once she heard the cook complaining that tradesmen were refusing to supply any more goods until their bills were paid. Once, as she left the house, her arm was seized roughly by a man lurking in a doorway, who demanded to know if Lady Stretton was in the house.

'No, she's visiting friends,' Rose told him.

He released her arm and stood scowling.

'What do you want with her?' Rose enquired curiously.

'I want my money,' he returned shortly. 'Either she pays me or I'll strip the fine clothes I made her off her back. If she's not careful, Lady Stretton is going to take her fine airs and graces to a debtors' prison.

A housemaid laughed at her naïveté when she mentioned this incident.

'The footmen would soon deal with him if he tried to get near my lady.'

'But why doesn't Lady Stretton pay her bills?' Rose asked timidly.

The housemaid gave her a pitying look.

'With what? Lord Stretton made sure that he took her jewels and everything else of value with him when he went to France. She is wildly extravagant, whether she has the money to pay for what she wants or not.'

'Then she'll be ruined.'

The other girl shrugged carelessly.

'She would have been by now, but so far she's managed to persuade her brother, Lord Wilde, to help her from time to time.'

'Aren't you worried about your wages?' Rose asked, remembering what John Stubbs had said.

'I make sure I get them in goods or kind, even if I don't get money,' the housemaid said firmly. 'If you've any sense you'll do the same.'

She left Rose puzzled and worried. She would not stoop to petty theft, but she had to get money somehow. All this was forgotten, however, at least for the time being, when Lord Wilde suddenly arrived.

Rose came back one Sunday after being to church to hear a popular minister preach and found the house in an uproar. Pure wax candles were being lit generously throughout rooms which were usually sparingly lit with tallow unless there were guests. The best dishes and wines were being brought forth, and the remaining silver and glasses were being hurriedly polished by servants who for once seemed eager to work.

'Lord Wilde is here,' she was informed by a breathless maid who was hurrying upstairs with her arms full of white linen. 'You'd best hurry to help her ladyship. She's been calling for you for some time!'

Rose picked up her skirts and fled up the stairs, aware that Lady Stretton could flare up in ugly little gusts of temper if her wants were not satisfied immediately. She paused outside her ladyship's room, straightened her cap, and then tapped on the door. When a voice called to her to enter, she found there was no reason to fear tantrums from Lady Stretton who was lying back on a couch, carelessly wrapped in a loose gown, and laughing happily at the man who lounged gracefully against a table.

As the two faces turned towards Rose, she was struck by how similar they were. Both had the same straight black hair and vivid blue eyes, the same proud tilt of the head. For some reason she had imagined Lord Wilde as a man of middle-age, but now she was dazzled by an extremely handsome man who could not have been more than thirty.

'Come in, child!' Lady Stretton welcomed her, stretching out one white arm languorously. 'I've been telling my brother what a treasure I found in the wilds of Cheshire.'

Rose approached shyly, bobbed a curtsy, and looked up from under her lashes to see Lord Wilde looking at her with frank appreciation.

'A very pretty blossom,' he commented, and paused to admire the blush that rose in response in her smooth cheeks.

'You're embarrassing the poor girl, Nigel,' Lady Stretton scolded him lightly. 'Go away and let her get me ready for dinner.'

Her brother gave a mock bow.

'If you insist, though I'd rather stay.'

He looked back when he reached the door and caught Rose gazing after him, rewarding her with a quick, intimate smile that made her blush again.

'A charming man!' Lady Stretton commented as she settled herself in a chair before the mirror and waited for Rose to dress her hair. 'Don't you think he's very handsome?'

'Indeed he is, my lady,' Rose agreed

warmly, and then added, 'You and he look very alike.'

Lady Stretton accepted the compliment with a smug smile.

'Is your brother staying long?' Rose dared to ask, wondering whether she would have another meeting with the good-looking and gracious lord.

'For a few days,' was the reply. 'He has affairs to see to in London. Do you like what you have seen of him?'

This question came sharply, and she was looking attentively at Rose's face as it was reflected in the mirror.

'Yes, indeed!' Rose said with spontaneous enthusiasm, and a smile curled Lady Stretton's lips.

'Be nice to my brother,' she said in a tone that held almost a hint of warning. 'His friendship could be very rewarding.'

Rose nodded and busied herself with her work, wondering what her ladyship meant, and deciding that she was being informed tactfully that his lordship could prove generous to good servants.

Whatever Lord Wilde's affairs in London were, they occupied much of his time and followed an erratic pattern. Sometimes he left early in the morning and his servants were still waiting up for him when the rest of the household retired to bed. Sometimes visitors who seemed anxious to avoid being seen came to him, and he would be closeted with them in his rooms for hours.

Rose never knew when she would meet him. Sometimes he was with his sister, at other times she would encounter him in the maze of passageways or find him writing in the library. Wherever it was, he would greet her with the same quick smile that made her feel he knew her well, even if they had scarcely exchanged a dozen sentences. Once, as they met by a window, he came close and with one finger tipped up her chin so that he could scrutinise her carefully.

'A flawless beauty,' he said slowly, and then stepped back from her and walked away when he heard another servant approaching.

The next day he sought her out as she sat mending linen alone in the housekeeper's room.

'My lord!' she said, trying to rise at the same time as she tried to keep hold of her needle and the voluminous folds of fabric.

He gestured to her to sit, laid something on the table beside her, and left without a word. When she picked up his gift she found it was one perfect rose held in a silver holder. Her eyes widened. What a perfect present, a beautiful wordless compliment! How much more gracious to give her this small silver work of art than a handful of coins!

She did not see him the next day, but her imagination was hard at work. Lord Wilde clearly admired her. Could it be more than that? There was such a thing as love at first sight, after all. She wondered if the excitement she felt whenever she saw him, the way her pulse raced and her cheeks burned, were symptoms of love. She had certainly never felt anything like this when Richard was courting her.

Rose found that she even dared to have dreams of herself as his wife, Lady Wilde. Why not? His wealth would make her lack of dowry unimportant. She would be Lady Stretton's sister-in-law, and that elegant lady would help her take her place in Society. With Lord Wilde's money she could keep her mother in comfort, free from all worries and very proud of her daughter's fine husband.

Hanging up Lady Stretton's gowns, Rose stroked the silk and velvet fabrics and looked enviously at the glowing colours. If she became Lady Wilde she would wear such fine clothes. And Richard Overton? Here the dream nearly vanished. She was aware of how desperately unhappy he would be if she married someone else. But they had never been properly promised to each other, she argued with herself, and surely he would recognise that a plain, Cheshire farmer was no rival to a rich, handsome nobleman.

She sighed and shook her head, telling herself not to be so stupid. Lord Wilde was a gentleman who appreciated the sight of a pretty face and enjoyed a little flirtation, but that was all. The gulf between him and his sister's maid was too great to bridge. This was no fairy tale.

She busied herself with various tasks, eager to distract her thoughts, only to have all her good resolutions collapse the next day when she was summoned to Lady Stretton's room to find no sign of her ladyship but with her brother waiting in the middle of the room. She looked at him in surprise, but he smiled and beckoned to her.

'Come in and shut the door, Rose. My sister will be here in a few minutes.'

She moved forward and shut the door obediently, but hovered near it uneasily until he advanced and took her by the hand to lead her farther into the room.

'I must admit to a small lie, Rose. I said my sister required your attendance, when in fact it was I who wanted to see you.'

As she tried to release her hand he held it more tightly.

'I'm tired of only meeting you by chance for a few seconds, so I thought of this way to have you to myself for a little while.'

'My lord,' she stammered, 'it is not fitting. The other servants will gossip.'

There was a quick look of angry haughtiness.

'I decide what is fitting in this house, Rose.'

His voice softened again.

'Did you like the gift I gave you? I have another.'

He held out his free hand and opened it, palm uppermost. On it rested a small gold ring. Rose forgot her scruples and gazed at it wide-eyed.

'I can't take that!'

'Of course you can,' he said softly, lifting the hand he had imprisoned.

She watched, spellbound, as he slipped the ring on her finger.

'You know what this means, don't you, Rose?' he murmured.

She gazed at him, her mind in too much confusion to speak, aware of his arm going round her and his face above hers. Not even Richard had kissed her on the lips! She closed her eyes and held up her face expectantly, and heard a soft laugh.

'Not now, Rose. Wait till I can show you properly how much I want you.'

She stood bewildered as he released her. As he left the room he met Lady Stretton in the passage. She looked at him enquiringly and he answered with a triumphant smile and a nod. Her ladyship looked very complacent when she went into the room and appeared not to notice Rose's new adornment.

Lady Stretton apparently had nothing much for Rose to do at that time and the girl fled to the sanctuary of her own room where she sat on her bed, eyes shining, convinced that her wild dreams were coming true after all. She stretched out her hand and surveyed the ring. Lord Wilde must love her, and the proof was that he had put the ring on the third finger of her left hand, and everyone knew that finger was linked to the heart! Unable to keep still under the press of her emotions, she pirouetted happily round the room.

Soon, very soon, he would tell her he loved her and wanted her to be his wife. Till then she would have to keep the ring hidden away from the prying eyes of other servants. It hurt her to have to take the sign of his love from her finger, but soon the whole world would know!

It was a severe blow to find that Lord Wilde had left the house early the next morning and had not returned by bedtime. Rose's duties were poorly done that day, for her mind was on other things, on her glorious future. A day's delay did not matter, she told herself in consolation, when there were years before them. At night she lay awake, straining to hear noises that would mean he had returned. Finally she fell asleep, her cheek resting on her left hand where she wore his ring.

She woke suddenly in alarm. There was a noise at her door, the sound of a key turning in the lock. But she had locked the door as she always did! Who had another key? As she scrambled desperately out of bed on the far side away from the door, a line of candlelight widened as the door was opened gradually and she saw from the light he carried that the figure in the doorway was Lord Wilde. He peered forward into the darkened room.

'Rose?'

She moved slightly and he heard the rustle of linen and chuckled slightly.

'There you are!'

He stepped into the room and closed the door behind him.

'I've come to seek your company.'

Overwhelming disillusionment kept her still for a second, but then her fingers closed on the solid pewter candlestick. Rose Kingsley, respectable farmer's daughter, would fight for her honour.

'If you take one step nearer, I'll strike you! Get out of my room!'

He stopped, evidently puzzled.

'What are you talking about? You expected me, didn't you? You took my presents.'

There was a slight slurring of his words that told her he was at least partly drunk.

'I didn't realise what you wanted in return!'

'Now you do. I want you and I've paid in advance.'

He set down his candle and started towards her, only to halt abruptly as she hurled the heavy candlestick at him, hitting him in the upper body. He doubled over, cursing, and then as she tried to edge round him so that she could reach the door and call for help he grabbed at her. She nearly fell, then lashed out desperately at him with her fists. He seized a wrist, only to have her tear desperately at his face with her nails until he yelled with pain and pushed her away. She seized the fallen candlestick and stood facing him.

'I'll kill you!' she warned, glaring at his distorted, bleeding face.

He took a lurching step towards her and she raised the candlestick threateningly. He halted in his tracks. The charm had vanished, and the good looks were temporarily ruined.

'You took my ring!' he hissed.

She pulled the ring from her finger and threw it at him.

'You can take it back! If not a token of true love it means nothing to me.'

He lifted an arm as if to strike her, but saw the candlestick rise again.

'I will have you!' he said furiously. 'You were meant for me!'

Now it was her turn to advance, holding the candlestick menacingly, until his nerve broke and he snatched up his candle and bolted through the door. With urgent haste she locked the door again and pushed the chest which held her clothes against it before she felt safe enough to return to her bed, where she lay awake all night clutching the pewter stick.

In the morning she was tapping at Lady Stretton's bedchamber as early as she dared. Her ladyship opened her eyes and stretched languidly as the bed curtains were pulled back. At the sight of Rose's white face and shadowed eyes she seemed amused.

'Didn't you sleep last night, girl?'

Rose was almost sobbing.

'Your brother woke me. He came to my room.'

Her ladyship lay back on the pillows, apparently unsurprised by this news. Rose tried again.

'You don't understand, your ladyship! He tried to take me! I had to defend myself, to hit him and threaten to kill him, before he would go!'

Her ladyship sat bolt upright, glaring incredulously at Rose.

'You drove my brother from your room?'

Rose closed her eyes gratefully. Whatever happened between brother and sister, at least Lady Stretton would now protect her. Lady Stretton was out of her bed, throwing her wrap on. Then she turned on Rose.

'You stupid girl! Why do you think I brought you to London? You were my gift to my brother!'

6

Rose retreated before the woman's fury, whispering in disbelief, 'What do you mean? You needed a lady's maid!'

Lady Stretton sneered.

'London is full of women I could have hired as my maid, women with far more experience and talent than a raw country girl! Haven't you realised by now that I'm desperate for money? Haven't the other servants told you? My only hope was that my brother would help me, but when I appealed to him he told me he was tired of paying my debts and would not give me any more money. But I know his weakness for young girls and you were my bribe to him. In exchange for you he might have paid some of what I owe.'

She waved clenched fists above her head.

'But you, a peasant girl from a hovel,

you smiled and blushed at my brother and ogled him as if you were his for the taking, and then when he did you the honour to come to your room you attacked him! After you had encouraged him so blatantly!'

Rose defended herself indignantly.

'I liked him, and he gave me a flower-holder and a gold ring, but I thought he was being kind to me! I didn't know he was trying to buy me!'

Lady Stretton's eyes glittered, but she regained some self-control.

'I know what he gave you, because the trinkets were mine. Where are they now?'

'In my room,' Rose stammered. 'The flower-holder is by my bed, and I threw the ring at him last night, so it's somewhere on the floor. I'll fetch them and give them back to you.'

Abruptly, before Rose could move to do this, Lady Stretton ran to the door, threw it open, and raised her voice in a strident summons.

'John! Edward! To me at once!'

In seconds the two footmen she had called appeared, still hastily pulling on their jackets. She pointed dramatically at Rose.

'That girl is a thief. She has stolen a gold ring and a silver trinket from me. Take her to her room and I'll prove it.'

'That's not true!' Rose cried indignantly, but the footmen ignored her protests, seizing her and dragging her to her room, where Lady Stretton pounced triumphantly on the flower-holder and soon found the ring glittering in a corner.

'Look! These are what she stole from me!'

'What shall we do with her, my lady?' one of the footmen queried.

'Lock her in here,' she ordered. 'I shall decide her fate later.'

Locked alone in her room, Rose first wept and then raged furiously against the woman who had deceived her. Somehow she would show the world what Lady Stretton was really like! But the door was solid and locked firmly, and the small window was high above the ground. Time passed and no one came. Rose had not eaten that morning, and by late afternoon she realised that her ladyship had either overlooked the matter of food for the prisoner or was deliberately keeping her hungry. When a brisk knock came on her door she stood up eagerly, but the door did not open. Instead she heard Lady Stretton's voice.

'Mistress, are you listening?'

In spite of receiving no response she went on.

'I've given you time to think over the situation. Perhaps you don't realise what may happen to you. You are a thief, and my servants will bear witness to it. The law can punish you with whipping, transportation or even hanging.'

She paused again to let this sink in fully.

'However, I could be merciful. My brother left early today and will not return till tomorrow. If, when he does, you are prepared to return his favours, I may let him persuade me to forgive you.'

Rose stayed obstinately silent and Lady Stretton flared into sudden fury.

'We will see what another day's hunger does to your stubbornness! If you don't come to your senses then I will go to a magistrate and let the law take its course.'

Then she was gone, leaving Rose to wonder if she had the strength of will to continue to resist her threats. With nothing else to do, she went over every detail of the past twenty-four hours, sickened by her own stupidity. One small detail puzzled her. She was sure she had locked her door the previous night, yet as Lord Wilde had unlocked it later he must have had another key. Which key had been used to lock her in today?

Her bedclothes still lay tumbled as she had left them this morning, and feeling under the pillow, she found the door key which she had always kept safe there! She seized it with delight. Now she had the means to escape from her room, but could she then escape from the house? She had realised from the lack of noise outside the door that there was no servant posted as guard as they were evidently relying on the stout door to keep her in. But once outside, she would have to make her way down the staircase and try to find some way to leave the house, and every step would mean risking an encounter with a servant who would raise the alarm.

She sat down to think out her course of action. Of course she would have to make her attempt late at night when the servants were no longer about, but a young girl on her own would be at high risk from thieves and vagabonds if she were found wandering the streets in the middle of the night, and she wanted as much time as possible to get away from Stretton House before the search for her started.

Midnight, or a little earlier, would be the best time, and then she would be less likely to encounter servants if she went down the main staircase instead of the back staircase which led to the servants' hall. She knew some stayed up late, enjoying their mistress's wine cellar.

With something to plan and look forward to she felt much better, and even the hunger pangs seemed to grow less. Carefully she put together a few essentials in a bundle, counting out the pitifully few coins she had accumulated. Then all she could do was wait. The hours passed very slowly. Sitting alone with the dull ache of hunger always present, Rose wished passionately that she had never come to London. She had treated Richard Overton abominably, had known that as soon as she told him that she was going with Lady Stretton.

If she had stayed in Frotesham she would be betrothed to him by now and looking forward to her wedding. As it was, even if she ever managed to return there, it would probably be to find him betrothed to Alice Wright. But at least she would be at home with her mother among people she knew and could trust.

The light finally faded and Rose sat on in the dark, occasionally hearing noises of activity faintly through the door. She heard the sound of rain on the window panes. Well, at least that should keep the streets fairly empty. At last she calculated that it must be midnight, and her heart was thumping as she stood up, the key grasped in her hand. This was her only chance. If she were to be caught trying to escape, Lady Stretton would make sure that there would be no other opportunity.

Very slowly she turned the key in the lock and very slowly opened the door slightly, almost expecting a shout of discovery as it moved sufficiently for her to slip out. Carefully she drew it close behind her and re-locked it, pocketing the key. If she could get clear of the house, no one would know she was gone until they finally opened her bedroom door.

Very cautiously in the darkness she made her way to the head of the stairs, glad that at this level there were no creaking boards. Step by step she crept down to the first-floor landing. One more flight of stairs and then the main door would beckon her across the hallway. Except that it would probably be locked by now. In that case she would have to make her way out through one of the ground-floor windows, which could be opened from the inside.

Just as she was about to start down the final flight, she froze as there was a burst of noise and the hall below was suddenly lit up. Some servants had obviously stayed up late and were only now about to carry out their duties to lock up. If only she had left her room minutes earlier! Now she could identify voices. John Stubbs and Peter had lowered their voices to loud whispers, but she could still hear Peter assuring John that he would see to the doors.

Then she saw him come into the hall, carrying a small lantern in one hand and a large bunch of keys in the other. Rose saw him checking the windows and then he walked towards the front door. Standing still, hardly breathing, she suddenly realised that her bundle was slipping from under her arm. She gripped it tightly, hoping the sound of cloth on cloth caused by the small movement would not be heard.

Down below, Peter seemed to hesitate in the very act of putting the key in the first of the door locks. He stood up, looked round, and then peered up the stairs. It seemed to Rose that he was looking straight at her. Then, very deliberately, he turned and walked away from the still unlocked door, and the lantern light vanished. Quick as lightning Rose fled down the stairs and across the hall, tugged the door ajar and squeezed through. Seconds after she did so the door was pushed shut and she could hear the bolts being shot and keys being turned in the locks. Peter might have been too weak and fearful to try to help her during the day, but now he was giving her a chance of freedom.

Rose scurried along the road, keeping close to the walls so as to be as unnoticeable as possible. When she had turned a corner and was out of view of Stretton Place she paused, almost unable to believe that she had got away from the house. Most of London's residents were safely behind locked doors by now, and the great city seemed very dark and threatening to Rose. But her destination lay hundreds of miles to the north, and the sooner she started the sooner she would get there, she told herself sternly. She went very cautiously, slipping through the unlit streets like a shadow, crouching in doorways twice while noisy groups made their drunken way along the street.

Dawn found her very tired, but already on the outskirts of London among the market gardens which provided much of the city's fresh food.

She found a small hut and took shelter in it, wedging the door shut in case she should be disturbed, and then collapsed exhausted. She slept on till the late afternoon, when the wintry darkness was already falling, but she had regained some energy. Now she wanted food, and that she got from a gardener's wife who gave her supper and a bed in return for help with the cooking and a few chores.

The next day she trudged steadily onwards, and in the evening asked the woman in charge of a small wayside inn if she could work for her supper. The woman swung round impatiently.

'Don't bother me! I've no time for beggars now. There's too much to do.'

'I'm not a beggar,' Rose said steadily. 'I can clean and get food ready.'

The woman turned back to her, hands on hips, and considered her thoughtfully.

'Will you wash dishes?'

Rose nodded, and the woman sighed gustily.

'Well, I need help and I suppose you can't do much harm. Get into the kitchen.'

Rose toiled at the dishes and then went on to help the cook, who seemed to be preparing an unusual amount of food.

'You look as if you are going to feed an army,' she observed as she busily chopped carrots and onions.

'Well, isn't that what we're trying to do?' the retort came, and Rose looked at her in bewilderment.

'Don't you know?' the cook said in response to her surprise. 'General Monk is camped near here with seven thousand men. With a little luck a fair number of them will be calling here tonight and we'll make a fat profit.'

'I only left London two nights ago,' Rose explained. 'I've been in service there and now I'm on my way back to Cheshire to see my mother. Why are the soldiers here?'

The cook, busily bending over a pot,

shrugged expressively.

'Who knows? But General Monk has got more sense than most of the leaders who have been squabbling since Oliver Cromwell died.'

Well, it was nothing to do with Rose. While noise grew in the tap-room, she eagerly ate her supper in the kitchen, then dozed on a stool by the fire, waiting for the dirty supper dishes to be brought in. When the door swung open she stood up, ready to go to work again, but the cook was empty-handed, and behind her were two men in buff leather jackets — soldiers who strode up to Rose.

'Are you the girl who's recently been in London?' she was asked.

'Till two nights ago.'

'Then General Monk will be pleased to see you. Come with us.'

At this both Rose and the cook protested, but the men stood firm.

'General Monk wants all the news from London he can get.'

'You said you wanted to talk to the

girl, not to take her away!' the cook said indignantly.

'She'll be safe enough with us,' one soldier assured her, but the cook was not satisfied until the soldiers had agreed that her fourteen-year-old son could accompany them and see that Rose was well treated.

Escorted by the soldiers and the boy, Rose allowed herself to be conducted to a farmhouse which General Monk had commandeered for the night. Rose found herself face-to-face with a stoutish, middle-aged man seated at a table which was covered with maps and papers. Half-a-dozen officers were also in the room.

'General, you asked us to bring you anyone who had been in London in the last few days,' one of the soldiers told him. 'This servant girl left there two days ago.'

'A servant-girl? I doubt if she can give us much information,' Monk commented. 'However, we'll see. Who are you, and what have you been doing in London?'

'I have been lady's maid to Lady Stretton,' Rose began, and stopped, aware of the sudden silence, as she realised that not only General Monk but his officers were now focusing their attention on her.

'Lady Stretton!' Monk breathed. 'Did you see her brother, Lord Wilde, by any chance?'

'Yes. He is visiting his sister and has been for some days.'

'Two arch-conspirators,' Monk said heavily.

Then he began to question Rose closely about the movements of Lady Stretton and her brother, and also about any visitors to their house, while one of the officers made notes. Sometimes Monk was plainly disappointed by Rose's ignorance of details and identity, but other times he nodded enthusiastically and urged her to continue. It was an hour before the interrogation ended, and the cook's son was half-asleep in a corner by then.

'What do you want to know all this for?' Rose asked finally.

Monk gave her a grim smile.

'England is in disorder,' he said, 'and there are always creatures who seek opportunities to benefit when law and social order break down. Lady Stretton and Lord Wilde are such creatures.'

'And what do you plan to do?' Rose asked bluntly.

Some of the officers seemed to find this presumptuous, but Monk waved them to silence.

'I have seven thousand men under my command, the best-trained and best disciplined body in England. Soon I shall enter London with them and deal with the opportunists, the trouble-makers. Then it will be my task to bring peace and order back to this country.'

'Will you rule Britain, like Oliver Cromwell?'

He shook his head.

'There are others with older and better claims than me.'

'King Charles!'

He smiled, but did not commit himself further. Instead, he turned to Rose's own problems.

'What do you propose to do now, my girl?'

'Make my way to Cheshire and my home.'

'A long walk for a young girl on her own. I may be able to help you in return for your information. Two of my men will be riding for Chester in the morning with messages for my friends. They are a dependable, trustworthy pair, and if you would like to go with them I can assure you that you will be quite safe.'

Rose's eyes lit up and she thanked him gladly before she and the yawning cook's son were taken back to the inn.

Early the next morning, two troopers on horseback were at the inn door, but Rose was all ready to leave for her journey home.

As Monk had told her, the two troopers were fatherly men who treated

Rose like a daughter, and whether they spent the night at a private house or an inn, they made sure she was well looked after. Both had spent nearly twenty years of their life in the service of the army, and both were eager now to retire to a peaceful life in the country.

In a few days they crossed into Cheshire, and Rose was soon straining to see the outline of Frotesham Hill against the skyline. It seemed a long time till they actually reached the outskirts of the village, and the first person Rose recognised was Alice's father, Master Wright, as he leaned meditatively on a gate and watched the travellers approach.

She waved to him gaily from her seat behind one of the troops. The farmer frowned in surprise, peered at her from beneath his wide-brimmed hat, and then she saw his jaw drop with surprise. Then she forgot him and laughed with joy as her mother's cottage came into view. Soon she would see her mother and find out what had happened to

Richard Overton. Although so much seemed to have happened, she had in fact been gone for only a few weeks. Surely he could not have committed himself to Alice Wright already. Surely Rose still had a chance to win him back!

7

Mistress Kingsley held Rose tightly in her arms, weeping unrestrainedly. The two troopers had refused to break their journey when they were within a few miles of Chester, and mother and daughter had been left together to embrace and celebrate their reunion. When her first delight at Rose's unexpected reappearance had passed, Mistress Kingsley had had to listen in horror to her daughter's story of what happened in London to send her hurrying back to Cheshire.

'The woman is a corrupter, an evil creature, and everyone should know that!' she said fiercely, but Rose shook her head sadly.

'How can I prove what I told you? I doubt if she will pursue me this far, but she will tell everybody that I ran away from her because I was afraid that I would be punished as a thief, and it would be true. All I can do is hope that she forgets me and that I can carry on my life as I did before I met her.'

She bent to add another log to the fire, concealing the tears that stood in her own eyes. Already she knew that life could never be the same. Meeting her mother after the weeks of parting, Rose had seen how her mother was ageing. Instead of being her daughter's protector, Mistress Kingsley would soon be dependent on her youth and strength. Rose forced herself to turn back to her mother with a cheerful face.

'Tell me what has been happening while I was away. Have you seen anyone?'

Her mother hesitated.

'You know there are few people about at this time of the year,' she said evasively.

'You must have seen someone.'

'Mistress Smithson, and Susan as well.'

Rose could wait no longer.

'What about Richard?'

There was silence.

'Surely he came to see you, to ask if you had word of me, at least.'

Mistress Kingsley shook her head.

'He has not been near me. But he has been to Frotesham.'

'To the Wrights' farm?' Rose said resignedly.

'So Susan Smithson told me.'

Rose sank down on her chair and managed a wry smile.

'I've been a fool, haven't I? I jumped at the chance to go to London, thinking how glorious it would be there and how dull it would be to stay here and marry Richard. But London isn't a glorious place to a penniless servant, and now Richard has got over his infatuation for a silly young girl and gone back to the rich farmer's daughter who will make him a much more fitting wife.' To herself she added mentally, 'And I've robbed you of your last chance for a comfortable old age, Mother. Forgive me.'

At least it was comforting to go to bed in her own home. Rose lay awake, listening to the wind in the trees, and struggled to come to terms with what she had learned. All the long way home she had told herself how eager she was to see her mother again, but now she was aware just how much she had relied on finding Richard waiting for her. He had said he would always love her, but she had turned her back on him, straining his faith too hard.

The next day she stayed at the cottage, eagerly helping her mother with various tasks. Whenever she looked up from her work she was glad to look out on the Cheshire countryside instead of the narrow streets of London.

Market day followed, and Rose was looking forward to meeting her old friends and neighbours for a gossip. London might have been a great disappointment to her, but there was still plenty that she could tell Susan and the others about the great city and the different way of life there. Mistress

Kingsley, however, slept badly and woke in pain, troubled by rheumatism which had begun to afflict her, and decided to sit by her warm hearth and let her daughter go to market alone.

In spite of the cold February weather, there was the usual crowd and bustle about the stalls. After all, this was the weekly meeting place of the neighbourhood, as well as the main shopping event of the week. Rose soon saw an acquaintance of her mother's, another widow, and greeted her with a smile, only to see the woman return her greeting with an icy glare and turn away without a word. Puzzled and a little hurt, Rose went on to encounter similar reactions from two other women. What was the matter with them? Was there some jealousy of the girl who had escaped from the village, or, more likely, were they showing their disapproval for the way she had abandoned her mother?

Then she saw Mrs Smithson with Susan by her side, and called out a greeting to them. They must not have heard, for they hurried away in the opposite direction before she could reach them through the crowd. She was about to pursue them, but then they were forgotten at the sight of a familiar tall figure.

'Richard!'

He turned and saw her, and for a second her heart leaped at the joy and welcome on his face. Then, all emotion was wiped clean and he faced her with a cold, expressionless mask and made no move towards her. Impetuously she went up to him and seized his hands, but they were unresponsive. She gazed up at him in bewilderment.

'Richard, it's me! I've come back home. Aren't you glad to see me?'

'I trust you are well, Mistress Rose,' he said with no feeling.

Tears sprung to her eyes.

'Is that all you are going to say to me?'

Suddenly Alice Wright thrust herself between Rose and Richard, forcing

Rose to release his hands and step back.

'Why should he say more?' Alice said shrilly and loudly. 'A greeting is more than you deserve from any respectable man or woman, Rose Kingsley. Get back to your hovel of a cottage and hide your shame there!'

Rose stared at her disbelievingly, and then looked around in horror as murmurs of agreement came from the onlookers. Richard stood unmoving, his eyes fixed on Rose. The murmurs grew louder and uglier. Rose found herself growing slightly fearful. Someone jostled her hard from the back and she nearly fell. Then Richard strode to her side, glared at the offender and raised his voice commandingly.

'Have you forgotten what the Bible says? Let him who is without sin cast the first stone. There will be no violence here today! You should pray for her, not attack her! Now, let her leave!'

Confused and afraid, Rose still had her pride. With cheeks blazing and chin raised defiantly she walked steadily towards the ring of women who now surrounded her. Whatever had happened, whatever the explanation was for Richard's strange behaviour, she would not give these women the satisfaction of seeing her cry. Reluctantly they gave way before her and she walked on without a backward glance, out of the village, back to her mother.

Mistress Kingsley was as angry and bewildered as her daughter.

'They must all have gone mad!' she said, rheumatism forgotten in her fury. 'I shall go and ask Mistress Smithson what all this to-do is about.'

In spite of her daughter's protestations that she should stay in the warm, she wrapped herself up well and launched herself towards the Smithsons' home in fighting mood. When she came back an hour later, however, she was drooping sadly.

'What did she say?' Rose demanded, chafing her mother's cold hands as she sank into her chair.

Mistress Kingsley shook her head,

too overcome with emotion to speak for a time. When she did, it was with tears and lamentations.

'There are such wicked stories being told about you, Rose! It is being said that Lady Stretton turned you out as soon as you reached London, and that you have lived by selling your body, travelling the country with a set of soldiers as a common wench, a camp-follower.'

Rose shook her head in disbelief.

'But that is nonsense! What grounds have they for saying such things?'

She stopped suddenly.

'Master Wright! It's him! I saw him when the soldiers were bringing me home. But he would never invent such a story!'

'No, but his wife and daughter would,' Mistress Kingsley said, sitting up abruptly. 'Mistress Wright could always make a scandal out of the slightest happening. If her husband told her that he saw you riding with two soldiers that would be enough for her to make up a sorry tale!'

'And everybody likes a good scandal, of course,' Rose said. 'If Mistress Wright has been spreading those lies about me all yesterday there are plenty who will have believed her. But surely Richard did not believe her?'

Mistress Kingsley sighed despairingly.

'You hurt him very deeply, Rose, when you chose London and Lady Stretton rather than marriage with him. Alice Wright will have told him that her mother's wild guesses are facts, that she has proof of what she says.'

'What can I do?' Rose said helplessly. 'It is my word against hers, and I cannot prove my innocence. I was brought home by soldiers. They were two good, decent men, but they are gone now and cannot testify to the truth.'

'We wait,' her mother said finally. 'There is nothing else to do. If anyone dares to speak to me on the matter I shall soon put them right.'

'You mean you will tell them that instead of throwing me out Lady Stretton locked me in my room and accused me of being a thief?'

'All scandals fade in time,' was all the comfort her mother could offer. 'The village will find something else to talk about eventually.'

That night, Rose wondered to herself how long that would take. She lay awake remembering how Richard had looked at her, trying to take comfort from the way he had protected her from physical aggression and sent her safely homeward, but the comfort vanished as she was forced to accept the fact that he had believed Mistress Wright's slanderous stories.

The weather was miserably wet for the next few days, so when Mistress Kingsley and Rose saw no one during that time they could not be sure whether it was the cold rain that kept former friends away or whether the pair of them were being shunned because of Rose's ruined reputation.

A break in the weather did, however, bring a visit from Mistress Smithson. She knocked timidly at the door, obviously uncertain of her welcome, and indeed Mistress Kingsley greeted her old friend with cold disdain, grudgingly inviting her to enter the cottage only when it became clear that she would not go till she had had her say. Her manner was half-apologetic, half self-righteous when she was admitted.

'Mistress Wright was very sure of what she said,' she told them, 'and she is a woman of good standing in the village. Why should we doubt what she said?'

She glanced sideways at Rose.

'But then, at home, I began to think. I've known Rose since she was born, and she's always been a good girl. I told myself there must be some other reason why she's come back to Frotesham so soon, riding behind a soldier.'

She waited expectantly, while Rose and her mother looked at each other.

They both knew the danger of making unsupported allegations against a member of the family who owned most of Frotesham.

'London and Rose didn't suit,' Mistress Kingsley said finally. 'She was homesick for Cheshire, as well, so she left Lady Stretton's household. Then she met General Monk, one of Cromwell's generals, and because of some service she did him he sent her home with an escort of trusted soldiers.'

Mistress Smithson waited again, and then looked at them reproachfully.

'Is that all?'

'Isn't the truth enough?' Mistress Kingsley countered.

'Yes, but why didn't Lady Stretton send her home? How did she meet General Monk?'

These were questions that could not be answered without involving more questions which would inevitably reveal too much. Mistress Kingsley glared indignantly at her friend.

'You said you knew Rose was innocent, and yet now you want to know her every movement!'

Mistress Smithson stood up with some dignity.

'I trust her, but if you can't tell me, your oldest friend, what happened to her in London, then obviously I must feel that you are hiding something which can't be to her credit. I will give your daughter the benefit of the doubt, but you can't be surprised if others won't!'

When Rose and her mother still remained silent about the circumstances of her departure from London, Mistress Smithson swept out, plump figure expressing indignation.

The question of Rose and her possible guilt was hotly debated in Frotesham during the following days. There were those who preferred to believe the scandalous stories, and they were opposed by people like Mistress Smithson who had known Rose for years and refused to believe the more lurid tales. Some supported the Wrights because Master Wright was a well-to-do farmer whose local influence might affect their own well-being. Others detested Mistress Wright because they had suffered from her love of scandal-mongering in the past.

Meanwhile the Kingsleys got on with their life quietly.

One day Rose was out tending to the hens when Susan Smithson appeared, furtively beckoning to her from the hedge.

'Susan! Does this mean your mother has decided you won't be contaminated by speaking to me?' Rose said tartly.

Susan shook her head.

'Mother doesn't know I'm here. I just wanted to see you and talk to you.'

Rose put down the bucket of chicken feed and straightened up.

'If you hope to learn more about my time in London, you might as well go home now. I have good reasons to keep quiet, reasons that would shame others, not me.'

Susan resolutely made her way into the garden and embraced her friend.

'I know that! I'm longing to know what the reasons are, of course, but if you won't tell me I'll accept that you have good cause.'

For the first time in days, Rose felt tears rise to her eyes as she embraced her friend. Going into the cottage, they gossiped happily for the next hour. Susan listened eagerly while Rose told her about London and its fashions. Then it was Rose's time for questions.

'Have you seen Richard Overton?' she asked directly.

'Not since market day, when you spoke to him. Alice Wright speaks of him as if they are virtually betrothed, but he seems to be staying away from Frotesham now.'

'If you see him . . . '

Rose hesitated. Often during the wakeful nights she told herself that he should have had more faith in her, but what was the use of pride?

'If you see him, tell him that the

stories about me are lies. If he will come to see me, I will tell him the truth, all the truth.'

She looked pleadingly at Susan, who looked back with some embarrassment.

'If I see him, and if I can speak to him, I will tell him, Rose. But you know how unlikely it is that I will have the chance.'

To Rose, Susan's visit was a sign that normality might yet return to her life, but there were new troubles as well. She woke one rainy morning to find water dripping down one wall.

'The thatch will have to be repaired, Mother. I'll go up to Hawsby Hall and tell Michael Johnson about it.'

Her mother looked at her in despair.

'If Michael Johnson was still steward of the estate he might do something eventually, but he was dismissed after Lady Stretton's visit. Apparently she complained to the Earl of Dunsdale that he was incompetent and rude to her and he was dismissed. It was a cruel thing to do when he'd been a faithful servant for so long!'

'Then I'll see the new steward. What is he called?'

'John Trudworth, and I'll not let you go near him. He treats the estate and the hall as if they were his own. He's gathered a gang of ruffians about him and his one aim seems to be to extract as much money as he can from the tenants, though I doubt if the earl sees much of it.'

'Then let us hope for a dry season. Perhaps I can get up on the roof and patch it myself.'

8

Next day, Rose and her mother were disturbed by the sound of horses' hooves outside the cottage, and a rough voice shouting at the occupants to show themselves and be quick about it. Rose looked up in surprise from her sewing. Her mother stood and gestured to her to be quiet.

'It's John Trudworth, the new steward from the Hall,' she whispered. 'Stay here out of sight and I'll see what he wants.'

Outside, Mistress Kingsley stood with her back to the door. There was a trio of horsemen in the lane, which was not unusual when the steward called. John Trudworth had made himself so disliked nowadays that he rarely went anywhere without some of his followers as a bodyguard.

'You wanted to see me?' Mistress

Kingsley asked him.

He slouched in the saddle and stared down at her contemptuously.

'Not you, old woman. I've come to have a look at this pretty daughter of yours who's just come back from London.'

'My daughter is nothing to do with you,' she said sternly.

John Trudworth's face darkened.

'While you live here, she is one of my tenants,' he told her. 'Now, bring her out or I'll have my men drag her out.'

'There is no need for that. Here I am,' Rose said quietly, slipping through the door to stand close by her mother.

The steward looked her over so slowly and carefully that she felt like an animal being judged in a market. Then he grinned, showing tobacco-stained teeth in an unshaven face.

'It's true, you are pretty. And I hear you're willing to make a man happy.'

Mistress Kingsley started indignantly, but Rose clasped her hands and they stood together in silent dignity. The steward and his men laughed at them, mistaking it for the fear they loved to inspire.

'I'm on urgent business now, sweetheart,' John Trudworth told Rose. 'But don't worry. I'll be back,' and with a careless flourish of his whip he signalled the other two horsemen to follow him as he cantered off, leaving the two women very shaken as they went back indoors.

'This is more trouble because of Mistress Wright,' Rose fumed, then she kneeled to comfort her mother as she sat shivering with apprehension. 'Don't look so scared, Mother. I'll avoid him when I can and when I do encounter him I'll soon make it clear that he has been given the wrong impression of me.'

'You don't understand,' her mother wailed. 'He is man who takes what he wants, and we have no menfolk to defend you.'

'I can protect myself,' Rose said grimly, with a quick memory of the candlestick hitting Lord Wilde.

'But he is the earl's steward, and he has full power over the estate. If you anger him, he could have us evicted from this cottage.'

This was an unwelcome and very unpleasant thought.

'I'll do all I can to keep out of his way, Mother,' Rose promised. 'He can't quarrel with me if he never sees me.'

For some days Mistress Kingsley's fear seemed unjustified. The steward was busy elsewhere and never came near the cottage. Rose was inclined to believe that his visit had been a casual bit of cruelty, intended just to frighten the two women. Then, more than a week later, when her mother was at the market, John Trudworth returned, alone. Rose heard a knock on the door, which was thrust open before she could go to it, and the steward strode into the cottage and stood grinning at her.

'My mother is away, sir,' she said.

'I watched her go,' he said smugly.

She backed away as he came towards her.

'I believe you have been misled about me, Master Trudworth. I am no country slut for you to use.'

'I know that. You're a girl who's travelled and seen better places than this country hole. Maid in a noble household, I've heard, till you found a more amusing way to make a living,' he told her. 'I'm tired of living in a bachelor household in Hawsby Hall. I want you there as my housekeeper. It's a fine house, and you can have one of the best rooms, live like a lady.'

'I'm afraid I am unfitted to be a housekeeper.'

He laughed loudly.

'You don't want to be a servant again? I don't mind what you call yourself. Please me and you will be mistress of Hawsby Hall, as well as my woman. Shall we see if we are suited?'

He was very close now, reaching out for her. She brought up her right hand and slapped him across the face with all

143

her might, and he reeled backwards.

'I told you that you were mistaken in me!' she said fiercely.

With a roar he tried to seize her again, and this time her nails raked his face, drawing blood. As he clapped his hand to his face she grabbed a blackened iron that stood by the fireplace and lifted it threateningly.

'If you try and touch me I'll brain you!' she said fiercely.

He hesitated at her words and the look on her face. She advanced towards him with the improvised weapon raised, and could almost have laughed at the speed with which he made for the door and hastily climbed on the horse which was tethered by the gate.

'I'll be back!' he shouted, once he was safely out of her reach. 'You will be very sorry for this, and so will your mother, I promise!'

Rose's eyes were sparkling with fury when her mother returned. She told the older woman that John Trudworth had called and tried to be over-familiar, but she did not tell her mother about the violence she had used to get rid of him. Mistress Kingsley was upset enough by what she told her.

'Where could we go if we were evicted? Who would give us shelter? The Smithsons are tenant farmers and would hesitate to cross John Trudworth by taking us in. Anyway, they could not afford to feed two more mouths for long. If he comes again, couldn't you just smile and laugh a bit, pass his remarks off as jokes? It might keep him happy.'

Rose soothed her mother and assured her that she would do her best, at the same time sickeningly aware that it was too late for such behaviour to do any good.

John Trudworth arrived to get his vindictive revenge the following day. It was already past noon on a bitterly cold day with sleet mixing with the rain when the two women heard the noise of several horses and went out to see what it was. Rose saw that John Trudworth was the leader of four horsemen and two stout farm horses which were being led along by halters. In spite of the half-healed scars on his face where her nails had torn at him, the steward was grinning triumphantly. He halted his horse at the gate, where he took a document from his pocket and spoke directly to Mistress Kingsley, ignoring Rose.

'Do you recognise this, old woman? It's the agreement that was drawn up between you and old Michael Johnson when you moved to this cottage.'

'I remember. What's wrong? The rent is not due.'

'What is wrong, Mistress Kingsley, is that Michael Johnson was an old fool who couldn't do his job properly. This agreement is invalid.'

'But why? I thought it was the same as other agreements I have seen.'

Trudworth glared at her while keeping the paper out of her reach.

'Are you doubting what I say?'

'Then what must be done? I cannot

afford to pay more!'

Trudworth shook his head in mock sorrow.

'It's not that easy, I'm afraid. This was discovered because the estate has other plans for this plot of land. Now that we know you have no right to be here, which makes matters simpler, the cottage is to be demolished and the land cleared.'

Mistress Kingsley swayed as if she were about to faint, and Rose supported her desperately.

'You can't turn us out of our home!' she told Trudworth.

He leered at her triumphantly, his hand going up to his wounded face.

'But I can, Mistress Rose. Another time, make sure you don't offend someone with the power to do you harm.'

At this moment there was a distraction as Mistress Smithson and Susan were seen hurrying up the lane. Either curiosity or friendship had drawn them to the Kingsleys to see what was happening to their friends. Mistress Kingsley, with tears streaming down her face, wept in her old friend's arms as she told her of the threatened eviction, while Susan stood by in silent alarm. Rose faced John Trudworth. She could not believe that even he would threaten them like this. She would find the minister, seek help from farmers, get such a body of support that Trudworth would think again.

'How much notice are you giving us?' she asked, stony-faced.

His smile grew wider.

'None,' he said curtly, and turned to beckon forward his men and the farm horses. 'Fix the hooks and ropes to the roof-beam and harness up the horses,' he ordered.

Rose realised with sudden horror what he planned to do.

'Surely you're not going to pull the cottage down now?' she exclaimed.

'The sooner the better. Hurry up, lads.'

Her pride snapped.

'At least let us collect what little we can carry,' she entreated.

He did not bother to answer, busily directing the men to fasten the hooks and ropes to the beam and then to the horses. Mistress Kingsley had sunk to the ground, and Mistress Smithson was vainly trying to comfort her.

'We'll think of something, my dear. You and Rose can come to our house now and my husband will think of some plan.'

But Trudworth heard her.

'If you give shelter to these two, Mistress Smithson, I shall remember it and make sure that you pay for it!'

As Mistress Smithson hesitated, there was a shout from the men. They had fixed the ropes and were now shouting at the horses to pull. The great creatures took the strain, urged on by shouts and blows. The rope grew taut, and then suddenly there was a rumble as the roof beam of the cottage was pulled out of place. The roof sagged and collapsed, robbed of its support, and the walls of the building were partly demolished by falling timbers. When the dust and noise settled, the little cottage which had been home to Mistress Kingsley and Rose was reduced to a roofless ruin, and all that the two women had left in the world were the clothes they were wearing.

John Trudworth turned triumphantly to where Rose stood, white-faced, gazing at the pitiful remains of the dwelling.

'You're homeless beggars,' he told her brutally. 'This parish is not going to support you. Be on your way, and beg for a living!'

Rose stood as if turned to stone. She and her mother did not even have cloaks, and the icy rain was already soaking them. If they had to set off on foot now into the open countryside, when darkness was already falling, she knew her mother would be dead by morning. Rose would have died rather than surrender to Lord Wilde or John Trudworth, but did she have the right to sacrifice her mother? She looked hopelessly at the steward.

'You are wrong,' she said bleakly. 'We are not beggars. You offered me work at Hawsby Hall. I am prepared to accept that offer now.'

His jaw fell, and he stared at her incredulously, and then gave a bellow of laughter.

'See what it takes to bring some women to their senses! Do you mean it, or do you plan some trick?'

She shook her head resignedly.

'I will come to Hawsby Hall, on condition that my mother may stay with the Smithsons.'

'Agreed!'

'Then I will take her there now, with Mistress Smithson's help, and afterwards I will come to you at the hall.'

His face shone with malicious triumph.

'Be there within the hour, or my men will fetch you.'

She turned away without a word, and kneeled in the mud beside her mother.

With Mistress Smithson's help, she managed to get her to her feet and almost carry her to the Smithson's farm, Mistress Smithson wailing with distress at what had happened, Susan followed sadly behind. At the farm, Mistress Smithson was able to show her sympathy with practical action. Mistress Kingsley was rapidly stripped, dressed in a nightgown, and put in Susan's bed for the night. Master Smithson hovered downstairs, torn between pity and agitation for the safety of his own family. In the bedroom, Mistress Smithson looked across at Rose.

'Do you mean to go through with it?' she said softly.

'I must, if I am to save my mother. Most people in the village think I am a fallen woman already, so this will just confirm their opinion of me.'

Impulsively the farmer's wife threw her arms around her and kissed her.

'How can anyone call you a sinner when you are being forced into this by

John Trudworth?'

'You will find many people who will regard me as a hopeless sinner. Even the Wrights may feel justified.'

She returned the hug, grateful for the woman's kindness, and then bent to kiss her mother's semi-conscious face.

'I know you'll look after her. Now, if I may borrow a cloak, it's time I left for Hawsby Hall.'

Susan was nowhere to be seen. That was a pity, as she would have liked to say goodbye to her friend. Then, with a last farewell kiss from the farmer and his wife, she wrapped the borrowed cloak around her and set out for Hawsby Hall.

John Trudworth was waiting and threw the main door open when she arrived and welcomed her with a mocking bow.

'Welcome to your new home, Mistress Rose.'

She walked into the Hall, instinctively shrinking as she passed him so as to avoid his touch, and halted just inside the door to survey the scene, lit by candles set on the great table. When Michael Johnson had been steward the house had been cold and unaired, but at least it had been cleaned and tidy. Now it was dirty and untidy, with used dishes left carelessly around.

'It needs some care and attention,' Trudworth said airily. 'For some reason the womenfolk of Frotesham are reluctant to work here. Now you can put it in order.'

He was swaying slightly, and she realised that he was already slightly drunk.

'Now, I'll show you to your room,' he said, seizing a three-branched candle-stick from a chest.

'My lady's chamber, just as I promised. Now, it's time for my supper, and you'll serve that.'

'Please, first give me five minutes to make sure I have all I need.'

He shrugged.

'If you haven't, take what you want from the other rooms. The Earl of

Dunsdale isn't likely to come riding up to find out what's happening to his house.'

To her relief, he lurched out without further ado, and she stood for a minute in the centre of the room, nerving herself for the ordeal that was to come. She must think of her mother, not of herself. She served what cold meats, bread and cheese she could find in the kitchen. When he had filled his own plate John Trudworth insisted that she sit and share the meal.

'Usually my men eat with me,' he informed her, 'but I told them that tonight I wanted it to be just the two of us. They understood.'

He leered at her, and reached over to paw her arm. She forced herself to keep still.

'Where are they then?' she enquired.

'In the back part, the servants' quarters. It's where they sleep, anyway.'

Rose drank a little ale with her food, but Trudworth was steadily consuming neat brandy, and his speech was growing more slurred. When he finally pushed away his plate she stood up and began to clear the dishes, eager to escape from him even for a few minutes. He slumped back in his chair and grinned up at her.

'Nearly bedtime, my sweet. Leave those dishes in the kitchen and go up to your room. I'll just have another drink, and then I'll be with you.'

9

Rose sat on the edge of the four-poster bed, shivering uncontrollably, her arms wrapped round herself as she rocked backwards and forwards in misery. Suddenly she sat still and looked round the bedchamber, as dazed as if she had just woken from a deep sleep. It was as if the confusion of the last few hours had never been. She felt as if she had just come to her senses. Regardless of her mother, regardless of her own safety, she knew with certainty that she could not allow John Trudworth to lay a hand on her.

First of all she would have to escape from the house. Lord Wilde and John Trudworth, Stretton Place and Hawsby Hall, were very different, but for Rose the problem was the same. Safety lay in flight. She knew that it would be useless to appeal to Trudworth to let her go, but once away from him there must be something she could do. Would Trudworth and his men respect the sanctuary of the church if she could reach it? Could she steel Master Smithson to band together with other farmers against the steward? These were questions for later. First, she must get out of Hawsby Hall.

She would have to hurry. John Trudworth thankfully seemed to be lingering over his brandy a long time, but surely he would come to her room soon. Picking up the branched candlestick, Rose let herself out. The wind had been rising all evening, and draughts made the candles flare as she tiptoed to the point on the landing where she could peer down into the hall. Keeping hidden as much as possible, she craned her head to look.

Trudworth's head rested on his sprawled arms on the table. His rasping snores were audible even above the noise of the wind. He had drunk himself into a stupor! Hardly able to believe her good fortune, Rose ventured to stand up and lean over the oak banisters to confirm that he was in no condition to stop her leaving. Just at that moment a wild gust of wind drove stronger draughts through the house. The candles Rose held guttered, and then a flame, blown sideways, caught the dusty hangings on the wall which sheltered her from full view.

In an instant the dry fabric had caught fire and flames were racing up it. Rose tore at the hangings, beating the fire out with her bare hands. Below, Trudworth stirred, partly awoken by the noise. Abandoning discretion, Rose fled down the stairs and across the floor, only to find the door locked and bolted. Desperately she turned to a window and smashed the latch with the heavy candlestick, which she dropped as she forced the windows open and scrambled through into the wet, black storm.

She needed shelter, somewhere to plan her next move, and the only place she could think of was the great oak where Richard had stood watching her drive away in the coach. Seconds later, scrambling up into its network of branches, she remembered how she had once told Richard how she and Susan used to play in the centuries-old tree when they were children, spying on what was happening at the big house. If only he were here now!

At first she cowered down, sure that soon she would hear John Trudworth shouting to his men to pursue her. When all she could hear was the wind tearing through the trees, she dared to lift her head and look back at the hall. The sight made her sit up, forgetful of concealment. Through the upper windows of the hall a red glow could be seen, momentarily brightening into flames. The hangings must have been smouldering on in spite of her attempts to stop the fire, and the draught had fanned them to fresh, vigorous life.

Even as she watched, she could hear shouts of alarm. Trudworth's men had become aware that the hall was going up in flames and were out in the grounds, ready to deal with the catastrophe, but she could not hear Trudworth's voice. At least he would have other matters to think about than Rose for a time, and this was the perfect opportunity to get away unobserved. She slid to the ground, skinning her hands painfully, and turned to run, but at that moment strong arms seized her and a hand was roughly clapped about her mouth.

She was conscious of absolute despair. Trudworth must have traced her. Then her emotion changed instantly to incredulous delight when a low voice whispered, 'Rose?'

She stopped struggling and relaxed against her captor, aware of a moment's pure unexpected happiness.

'Richard! Why are you here?'

'To kill John Trudworth,' came the savage reply.

She found herself giggling hysterically. Solid, respectable Richard making threats of murder! His grip tightened painfully.

'Stop that silly noise and tell me what is happening!'

'I ran away, again! I couldn't bear the thought of John Trudworth even touching me, and when he drank himself senseless I managed to get out. But it seems I set fire to the house first!'

'Good!' he said curtly. 'From what I can see, those ruffians have let it get out of control, and nobody from Frotesham will come to help them, especially on a night like this. Let's be on our way before they think of looking for you.'

For a big man he was very light on his feet, guiding her skilfully under the lashing branches of the trees away from the blazing house.

'Where are we going?' she asked breathlessly as he hurried her along.

'The Smithsons' farm. I left my horse there.'

'Why did you come? How did you know I needed you?'

'Susan came to fetch me. I always

thought she was a light-headed lass, but she walked nearly six miles through this storm to get help for you. I took her back to her parents, left my horse there, and came in search of you. I was going to use the great oak as a look-out to spy on the house, as you said you did as a child, but instead I found you waiting there and the hall in flames. You don't seem in need of any help, after all my haste!'

'This is only the start of it, Richard. Oh, I've been such a fool and got myself in such a mess!'

'One thing at a time,' he told her. 'What I have to do now is get you somewhere safe for the night. We'll worry about Trudworth and the hall tomorrow.'

She stumbled on some obstacle, and suddenly found herself swept up in his arms.

'Lie still and let me carry you,' he ordered when she struggled in surprise, and she was grateful to stay in the protection of his arms until they reached the Smithsons' farmhouse where the family was waiting in high anxiety.

There, while Rose gratefully drank some mulled wine, Richard gave a brief account of what had happened.

'As Rose had the sense to set fire to the hall before running away, Trudworth and his men are going to be too busy to worry about her for some time. I will take Rose home to my mother's care. How is Mistress Kingsley?'

'Well enough,' Mistress Smithson assured him. 'I gave her a draught which will help her sleep. She is safe with us, but I think Rose should leave Frotesham tonight, as you suggest. We'll keep silent about everything that has happened today, for our own sake as well as Rose's.'

Soon Rose kissed her sleeping mother, hugged Susan in heartfelt gratitude, and found herself sitting in front of Richard on his familiar horse. As the Smithsons secured the door behind them, the couple set out on the ride to Richard's farm. The storm had almost blown itself out by now, and there were even glimpses of the moon between the scudding clouds. Rose rested happily in Richard's embrace.

'Why did Susan think you would come to help me?' she enquired sleepily, and felt him sigh.

'She said it was because she hoped I still loved you, and of course she was right.'

Rose gave a shaky laugh.

'Why should she think that after the way you behaved when we met at the market?'

His grip tightened convulsively.

'I was a fool that day! I met you scarcely an hour after Mistress Wright and Alice had been pouring out their poisonous tales about you. They claimed that they knew it was all true, that they would confirm it, and for a time I let myself be convinced. I suppose I wanted a reason to hate you after you had left me.'

Rose was quiet for a while.

'Have you changed your mind now?' she ventured.

He laughed ruefully.

'Yes, my love, even before you burned down Hawsby Hall rather than sleep with the steward. For two days after that scene in the market I was struggling to decide what I did believe. My mother saw that I was troubled and asked me what the matter was. I told her, and she told me roundly that I was a fool! She said that you might be light-headed and charmed away by dreams of London, but anybody with any sense could see you were a good, well-principled girl, and that Mistress Wright had always had a vicious, lying tongue. She was right, of course, and I knew it.'

'So what did you intend to do?' Rose whispered.

'Since that day I've been trying to get the courage to come and apologise to you, to ask you to forgive me, but I was afraid you'd turn me from your door and tell me never to come near you again. If only I had had the courage to come earlier! I could have saved you from what has happened today.'

Rose snuggled closer to him.

'I would have spoken very harshly to you, Richard, but I would have forgiven you, eventually. You always forgive the people you love.'

Richard halted the horse, and for the first time kissed Rose on the lips.

It was the early hours before a sleepy but happy Rose was entrusted to the care of Mistress Overton, who soon settled her snugly between white linen sheets given a welcome warmth by a warming-pan, and it was well into the next day before she awoke.

Mistress Overton had clearly been listening for the sound of her stirring, and bustled in with an armful of garments.

'Good morning, child. I've done what I could to find something to replace those rags you arrived in. We're about the same height, but I'm twice as wide as you, I'm afraid, but it's all I've got.'

When Rose came down dressed, her ample gown was gathered loosely in the middle. Mistress Overton tut-tutted but assured Rose that they would be able to alter some garments before long.

'Now, come and break your fast.'

Rose sat at the table obediently, but although she was fiercely hungry she wanted information first.

'Where is Richard?'

'Gone to Frotesham. You've probably forgotten that it's market day, so he'll soon learn all there is to know. Now, eat!'

Richard returned in the late afternoon. He looked tired, with shadows under his eyes, but he greeted Rose with a tender smile while his mother met him with a barrage of questions.

'First of all, your mother is fast recovering, Rose. I have said that tomorrow I'll drive the cart over to Frotesham and bring her back here. Now, if you'll get me some ale, Mother, we can all sit down and I'll tell you what I've learned,' he said firmly.

Sitting at the kitchen table, he seemed reluctant to start his tale, but Mistress Overton and Rose were eagerly waiting for him. In the end, he started abruptly.

'John Trudworth is dead. He was obviously too drunk to escape from the house and was killed by falling timbers before his men could break in.'

Rose was ashen-faced.

'I killed him!'

'Nonsense!' Mistress Overton said sharply. 'He was responsible for his own death. His lust and drunkenness killed him.'

'Don't feel guilty about the death of an evil man,' Richard added. 'If he had lived, I would have killed him myself.'

There was a pause before Mistress Overton said briskly, 'What else?'

Richard gave a savage smile.

'All good news. Hawsby Hall is destroyed. Trudworth's men knew that with their master dead there was no future for them in Frotesham, so they looted what they could from the hall, took the horses, and left. They've probably made for Wales, but that's no concern of ours. The important thing is that apart from the Smithsons, all those who knew that Rose promised Trudworth she would come to him at the hall are dead or gone, and that secret is safe with the Smithsons. The story I agreed on with them is that after Rose had rejected Trudworth and he had destroyed the Kingsleys' cottage out of spite, Rose and her mother took shelter at their farm and Susan brought me a message. I went to bring them both here. Mistress Kingsley was too ill to be moved, but Rose came with me.'

'Why did I leave my mother?'

'Because the Smithsons did not have room for the two of you, and although you were reluctant to leave your mother you knew Mistress Smithson would nurse her well, which she is doing.'

'A good story,' Mistress Overton said contentedly. 'The best part is, it is all true. It just leaves out Hawsby Hall.'

Rose fidgeted, eyes downcast.

'What's the matter?' Richard's mother enquired anxiously.

'It's just that people will ask why Richard should feel obliged to help us.'

Mistress Overton laughed scornfully.

'Is that all? Of course he'd come to help the girl he's going to marry!'

Rose was blushing deeply.

'But . . . '

'She means I haven't had a chance to ask her, Mother,' Richard interposed wryly.

Mistress Overton lifted her eyebrows.

'So? What's a few words? You are going to get married, aren't you? Well then, we saw the two of you had managed to meet and be reconciled some time during the last few days. Any other problems?'

'Yes,' Rose said heavily. 'I can't marry Richard when everybody thinks I'm a common wench. We would be shunned by his friends and neighbours. I will not ruin Richard's life.'

Mistress Overton had no reply ready

for this. The two women knew that in a small, rural community survival could depend on good relations with the people around you. They were shocked to hear Richard break into lighthearted laughter, and looked at him angrily. He held up his hands defensively.

'Wait till I tell you the rest of my news! Mistress Wright and Mistress Smithson met face to face in the market and Mistress Wright had the impudence to tell our friend that she should have nothing to do with the mother of a notorious loose woman. Mistress Smithson was in no mood to put up with that after the past twenty-four hours and she told Mistress Wright in front of nearly every woman in Frotesham that she was a liar. She said that if Mistress Wright had proof of your loose behaviour she should give it, and not just spread lurid stories about an innocent girl.

'It soon became clear that there was no such proof, and when Mistress Wright began to invent details she started to contradict herself. Sympathy was growing for you anyway, Rose, after people had heard that your cottage had been destroyed. In short, the scene ended with Mistress Wright thoroughly discredited and jeered. Now, will you marry me?'

'Of course,' Rose said simply.

He stretched a hand across the table and took hers in his warm clasp, while his mother looked from one to the other with great satisfaction.

'Well,' she said contentedly, 'if there are no more problems Rose and I will get on with the housework.'

10

Rose was weeding the little vegetable patch happily, under the spring sunshine of late April. The day was bright and warm, and everything in sight seemed lush and glowing with vivid colour. Through the open door she could hear the rattle of dishes as Mistress Overton busied herself with baking.

At first Rose had not been able to understand why Richard's mother, who had seemed to dislike her so much before she went to London, now treated her like a favourite daughter and was obviously looking forward to Rose's wedding with Richard which would take place in a few weeks' time. It was Richard who enlightened her.

'Mother likes to be needed. You and your mother seemed too self-sufficient and independent before. When you came here homeless and helpless with nothing left in the world, needing her help was the quickest way to her heart.'

Rose was sincerely grateful for the way Richard's mother had taken them in and nursed her mother back to health, and had grown truly fond of the older woman. Mistress Kingsley, though grateful, was still somewhat wary. She missed her old friends at Frotesham, and whenever Richard visited the village she would beg a lift on his horse and ride happily behind him to visit the Smithsons. At the moment she was staying there for a few days.

Rose looked with satisfaction at the tidy patch of ground she had covered and stood up, brushing the soil from her hands. Now the vegetable seeds could be planted.

'Can I help with the baking?' she asked Mistress Overton, having rinsed her hands under the pump in the yard.

Richard's mother looked round. She did not approve of idle hands, and one of the qualities she admired about Rose was her willingness to work.

'See how the bread dough is rising, and fetch me some more onions,' she instructed. 'Richard is working in the far field today, so I doubt if he'll come back till evening. We might as well do all we can.'

After carrying out these tasks, Rose chopped some sticks for the fire and then came in to share in the baking. The two worked companionably together, and Rose looked up in some surprise when a figure darkened the doorway. Had Richard come back early? But the elegant man who stood there wore clothes very different from Richard's serviceable garments. He also carried two pistols, now pointed at the women in the kitchen. Rose screamed, and Mistress Overton dropped the bowl she had been carrying.

'Lord Wilde!' Rose exclaimed.

Instinctively the two women drew together.

'I am glad you remember me,

Mistress Rose, after your sudden departure from my sister's house.'

Was he holding such a grudge against her that he had pursued her to Cheshire with the charge of theft?

'Of course you are wondering why I am here. Well, as your scream did not bring anybody running to help you, I assume there is no one else in the house. In that case I can explain.'

His voice and attitude were carefully casual, but the pistols were trained steadily on the women.

'I have it on reliable information, Mistress Rose, that you were the one who gave General Monk information about my sister and myself and the people I had been meeting. The general followed up the clues you provided, and as a result my sister and I are now fugitives, fleeing from the man who now controls England and who intends to act the kingmaker and hand it over to Charles Stuart in the near future. When my sister told me that we would pass near your home, I knew I must find you.'

Before he could go further, there was the sound of running footsteps and Lady Stretton appeared beside him. There was little sign of the carefully-groomed beauty they had first seen at the beginning of the year. Lady Stretton looked worn and haggard, a cloak clutched carelessly round her.

'Edward! Hurry up! Do what you came for and then let us go. If we linger here we will be caught!'

'Go back to the horses,' her brother told her sharply. 'We have a few minutes to spare.'

Rose, trusting that his sister was diverting his attention, moved a step towards the table, which still bore the sharp kitchen knives she had been using, but she saw a pistol barrel swing alertly towards her.

'Move away!' she was ordered. 'You, old woman, go and stand beside her near the fire.'

Mistress Overton, bewildered and scared, did as he ordered.

'What are you planning to do with us?' Rose demanded.

His smile bared his teeth.

'What do you expect? You rejected me, a personal insult, and now you have destroyed my life. I am going to kill you.'

Mistress Overton gave a wail of distress and Rose moved swiftly to stand in front of her, protecting her with her own body. Lord Wilde laughed.

'Brave but futile! I shall have to kill both of you, of course.'

Lady Stretton held out her hands entreatingly to her brother.

'Shoot them and be done with it. We must go. If we can't find a boat to Ireland before tomorrow we are done for!'

Her brother ignored her, and she hesitated briefly and then whirled round and ran out of the door. Lord Wilde's eyes were fastened on Rose, and she could see the beads of sweat on his face. Outside they could hear the thud of galloping hooves as Lady Stretton fled alone.

'A criminal about to be executed is allowed a few words before the end, Mistress Rose. I want you to beg my forgiveness for what you have done.'

If he was going to kill her anyway she would die with dignity. Rose pressed her lips together and shook her head. He took two menacing steps towards her.

'On your knees and beg me to forgive you!'

'If you are now facing justice because of what I did, then I am glad,' she said fiercely. 'If you kill me it will be murder, and I hope you hang for it.'

For a moment the pistols wavered and he seemed about to throw them aside and launch himself at her physically. Then the pistols steadied again, and she could see the knuckles of his right hand whiten as he tightened his grip and increased the pressure on the trigger. At that moment they all heard an incongruous little sound.

Someone was whistling happily as he came closer to the farmhouse. Richard had come home early after all! Rose saw Lord Wilde hesitate and cast a look over his shoulder, and she took a deep breath.

'Run, Richard! Run for your life!' she screamed, and pulled Mistress Overton down to the floor with her as Lord Wilde's pistol exploded.

Before he could fire the other pistol Richard burst into the room at full speed, and as he grasped Lord Wilde by the shoulder and spun him round, the pistol went off aimlessly and the ball buried itself in the ceiling. Then it was a ruthless hand-to-hand struggle between the two men. Richard was the taller and heavier, but Lord Wilde had agility as well as strength and was fighting for his freedom. While Mistress Overton crouched sobbing on the floor, Rose sprang up, reached for a kitchen knife, and watched bright-eyed for a chance to help Richard.

Her aid was not needed. Richard was

fighting to protect his womenfolk, regardless of his own danger, while Lord Wilde was trying to save his own skin. When the two men momentarily broke apart, Lord Wilde made a dash for the door. If he could reach his horse he could still follow his sister and escape. Before he could reach the open air, Richard was after him, within arm's length.

Edward Wilde saw the axe which Rose had used earlier on the sticks propped by the door and grasped it desperately. He swung it at Richard, who twisted away barely in time, but the momentum of the swing threw Wilde off balance. He dropped the axe, and at that moment Richard's fist, with all the power of his anger behind it, hit Edward Wilde's jaw and snapped his head back. The force of the blow knocked him off his feet, and he landed spread-eagled on his back on the stone floor.

'Get up!' Richard ordered, but the man lay unmoving. 'Get up!'

There was no response. Rose moved slowly towards the still figure.

'He's not breathing,' she murmured. 'His neck seems twisted.'

Urgently Richard kneeled by Lord Wilde and looked at him closely. Then he stood up heavily by the side of his enemy.

'He's dead. His neck is broken.'

Rose burst into tears. Richard took her in his arms, and then both of them had to turn their attention to Mistress Overton, who for the only time in her life, gave way to a fit of hysterics. The two young people sat her in her chair and tried to comfort her, momentarily oblivious to the body on the floor and the open doorway. As Richard's mother grew calmer, Rose became aware again of the problems that faced them.

'What happens now?'

'I think I shall decide that,' an incisive voice said.

The three stared at the newcomer in the doorway. His buff jerkin and scarlet sash proclaimed the military man. He was unarmed, however, unlike the two men behind him who stood stolidly with their pistols in their hands. The newcomer swept off his broad-brimmed hat and bowed to the two women and Richard.

'I gather that this is Overton Farm, and you must be Richard Overton and that lady your mother. In that case I must assume the other lady is Mistress Rose Kingsley.'

He strolled farther into the room and looked down at the body of Lord Wilde.

'My name is Captain Newton, and my men and I were in pursuit of this traitor and his sister. What happened to him?'

'He threatened Rose and my mother, so I attacked him. He was killed in the fight,' Richard said defiantly.

The captain showed no surprise.

'When we were trying to follow his path after Frotesham, a farmer's wife said she was afraid he might come here looking for vengeance. Instead he found his death at your hands.'

'I am not sorry I killed him, whatever the punishment,' Richard said harshly.

The captain beckoned one of his men.

'Find a horse blanket and wrap the body in it. We will take it to Chester.'

'Are you taking me as well?' Richard demanded.

The captain smiled and shook his head.

'Why should I do that? Edward Wilde called at this farm for some reason, to ask for some water, shall we say? Then, somehow, he met with an accident.'

Richard looked at him in bewilderment, and the captain clapped him on the shoulder.

'Do you think you are the only person who wanted Wilde dead? He has betrayed everybody, and if we had taken him alive he would have stood trial and then inevitably he would have been found guilty and executed. This way the state is saved some expense and he will have a more honourable burial than he deserves.'

At this moment another soldier shouldered his way into the room and muttered something to Captain Newton.

'Lady Stretton has been captured and is now on her way to Chester,' he said with satisfaction.

'What will happen to her?' Rose asked anxiously.

In spite of the wrong she had suffered, she was distressed by the idea of Lady Stretton possibly facing execution. Captain Newton smiled at her understandingly.

'Don't worry. She was only a fool, led along by her brother. She'll probably be shipped abroad to find shelter with any friends she may have. In fact the lady may be so desperate that she may be forced to return to her husband!'

Lord Wilde's body was being carried out and the captain prepared to follow it.

'Forget what has happened,' he advised them. 'Lord Wilde and his sister will not cause you any more trouble.'

Then he and his men were gone, the sound of their horses rapidly fading away, leaving Rose and the Overtons to cope with the aftermath of the scene. In fact it was Mistress Overton who seemed to return to normality first, suddenly aware of a smell of burning.

'My pies!' she exclaimed. 'Everything will be ruined!'

As Richard restored order in the room, Rose helped Mistress Overton deal with the ruined baking, but when this was done she slipped out into the garden. After a while Richard followed her and found her sitting sadly underneath an apple tree.

'I can't marry you, Richard,' she said abruptly as he approached. 'I bring bad luck. It was because of me that John Trudworth died in the fire, and Lord Wilde would not have come here to his death if it had not been for me.'

Richard sat down beside her and gently put his arm round her.

'They were responsible for their own deaths,' he told her. 'Men like them carry their own bad luck and destroy themselves.'

Rose gazed at him wistfully.

'I wish I could believe you. I don't want to bring you harm.'

'The only way you could destroy me now would be by refusing to become my wife. Trust me,' he said. 'Trust me now and in the years that lie before us.'

She was silent for some time, then looked up at him with tears on her lashes.

'I do, and I will always.'

He smiled down at her, tenderly wiping away the tears with his finger.

'Then there is nothing to fear.'

THE END

We do hope that you have enjoyed reading this large print book.

Did you know that all of our titles are available for purchase?

We publish a wide range of high quality large print books including:
Romances, Mysteries, Classics
General Fiction
Non Fiction and Westerns

Special interest titles available in large print are:
The Little Oxford Dictionary
Music Book, Song Book
Hymn Book, Service Book

Also available from us courtesy of Oxford University Press:
Young Readers' Dictionary
(large print edition)
Young Readers' Thesaurus
(large print edition)

For further information or a free brochure, please contact us at:
Ulverscroft Large Print Books Ltd.,
The Green, Bradgate Road, Anstey,
Leicester, LE7 7FU, England.
Tel: (00 44) **0116 236 4325**
Fax: (00 44) **0116 234 0205**

CONVALESCENT HEART

Lynne Collins

They called Romily the Snow Queen, but once she had been all fire and passion, kindled into loving by a man's kiss and sure it would last a lifetime. She still believed it would, for her. It had lasted only a few months for the man who had stormed into her heart. After Greg, how could she trust any man again? So was it likely that surgeon Jake Conway could pierce the icy armour that the lovely ward sister had wrapped about her emotions?

TOO MANY LOVES

Juliet Gray

Justin Caldwell, a famous personality of stage and screen, was blessed with good looks and charm that few women could resist. Stacy was a newcomer to England and she was not impressed by the handsome stranger; she thought him arrogant, ill-mannered and detestable. By the time that Justin desired to begin again on a new footing it was much too late to redeem himself in her eyes, for there had been too many loves in his life.

MYSTERY AT MELBECK

Gillian Kaye

Meg Bowering goes to Melbeck House in the Yorkshire Dales to nurse the rich, elderly Mrs Peacock. She likes her patient and is immediately attracted to Mrs Peacock's nephew and heir, Geoffrey, who farms nearby. But Geoffrey is a gambling man and Meg could never have foreseen the dreadful chain of events which follow. Throughout her ordeal, she is helped by the local vicar, Andrew Sheratt, and she soon discovers where her heart really lies.

HEART UNDER SIEGE

Joy St Clair

Gemma had no interest in men — which was how she had acquired the job of companion/secretary to Mrs Prescott in Kentucky. The old lady had stipulated that she wanted someone who would not want to rush off and get married. But why was the infuriating Shade Lambert so sceptical about it? Gemma was determined to prove to him that she meant what she said about remaining single — but all she proved was that she was far from immune to his devastating attraction!

HOME IS WHERE THE HEART IS

Mavis Thomas

Venetia had loved her husband dearly. Now she and their small daughter were living alone in a beautiful, empty home. Seeking fresh horizons in a Northern seaside town, Venetia finds deep interest in work with a Day Centre for the Elderly — and two very different men. If ever she could rediscover love, would Terry bring it with his caring, healing laughter? Or would it be Jay, the once well-known singer now at the final crossroads of his troubled career?